ASK AGAIN LATER

LIZ CZUKAS

HARPER TEEN
An Imprint of HarperCollinsPublishers

HarperTeen is an imprint of HarperCollins Publishers.

Ask Again Later
Copyright © 2014 by Liz Czukas
All rights reserved. Printed in the United States of America. No part of this
book may be used or reproduced in any manner whatsoever without written
permission except in the case of brief quotations embodied in critical articles
and reviews. For information address HarperCollins Children's Books, a divi-
sion of HarperCollins Publishers, 10 East 53rd Street, New York, NY 10022.
www.epicreads.com

Library of Congress Cataloging-in-Publication Data
Czukas, Liz.
    Ask again later / Liz Czukas. — First edition.
        pages   cm
    Summary: Instead of a "No Drama Prom-a" with a group of friends,
seventeen-year-old Heart LaCoeur must choose between two boys with good
reasons for asking her, but a flip of a coin leads not to one date but two complete—and very different—prom nights.
    ISBN 978-0-06-227239-3 (pbk.)
    [1. Proms—Fiction.   2. Dating (Social customs)—Fiction.]   I. Title.
PZ7.C9993Ask 2014   2013005073
[Fic]—dc23   CIP
                                                                    AC

Typography by Torborg Davern
14 15 16 17 18 LP/RRDH 10 9 8 7 6 5 4 3 2 1

First Edition

To Peg Grafwallner,
Terry McGinn, and especially
Tim Grandy

PART 1

call it in
the air

Two Weeks Before Prom

1 In which I introduce myself

Before she left, my mom gave me three things: (I) her wedding ring, (2) a closet full of kick-ass vintage clothing, and (3) the worst name in the world. The ring I keep in the shoe box under my bed, because seriously, a seventeen-year-old wearing a wedding ring? That's just weird. The clothing makes up the foundation of my wardrobe. And the name I'm changing as soon as I'm eighteen, because no one should have to go through life named Heart LaCoeur.

I know, right? You're probably thinking I'm a porn star, or a stripper. Maybe a romance novelist, if you're feeling generous. But I'm just a high school student with a lust for Broadway musicals and an unhealthy relationship with *The Big Book of Baby Names*. My copy is dog-eared, highlighted, and Sharpied into complete submission. I've got less than a year to go until I can march my butt down to the courthouse and choose my very own name for the rest of my life. Right now I'm leaning toward Audrey, after Audrey Hepburn, or Brigitte after Brigitte Bardot.

Sometimes, people ask me what it's like to be named Heart, but how am I supposed to answer that? I mean, how would you answer if a fish popped out of a lake and asked you what it was like to breathe oxygen? Apart from freaking out that a fish was talking to you, of course. You don't know what it's like to breathe anything else. You'd probably be like, "I don't know. It's okay, I guess. What's it like to breathe water, Talking Fish?"

But this is not a story about talking fish.

It's a story about prom.

I already had a date to prom—seven of them, actually, since I was going with a big group of friends. We'd dubbed ourselves the No Drama Prom-a Crew. Our entire goal for the night was to have fun, and not sweat all the clichés, like backseat-virginity-losing and ill-gotten beer. No thank you. No date, no drama, and my killer vintage lavender gown were my idea of prom perfection.

Then Ryan messed it all up.

2 During which I receive my first unexpected invitation to prom

It is a universal truth that a person cannot run in clogs, but that didn't stop me from trying. I was already late for play practice, and I knew from experience that the great and powerful director, Len Greenwich, did not think inappropriate footwear was a valid excuse. It finally occurred to me in the last fifty yards that I would probably move a lot faster if I just took off my shoes. Not to mention I was much quieter in bare feet.

I eased open one of the auditorium's doors and peeked through. In an amazing stroke of luck, Greenwich was onstage, his back to me. I seized the moment and scurried up the side aisle to join my friends in the first few rows.

"You're late," Lisa sang under her breath, looking at me out of the corners of her dark eyes.

"Gee, really?" I made a face as I squeezed past her to

get an empty seat farther down the row.

"Spleen." Schroeder greeted me with an extended fist, as I practically collapsed into the seat beside him. He never called me by my real name, always by some other internal organ. His favorites lately had been Pancreas and Lung. This may have been some type of misguided come-uppance on his part, as I refused to call him by his real name—Chase. But at least me calling him Schroeder is less disgusting than being called Spleen. And it's because he has blond hair, and plays the piano, like that kid from the Snoopy cartoons. Plus, his last name is Schaefer. How could I resist?

I bumped my knuckles into his—a little harder than strictly necessary. "Did I miss anything?"

"Yeah, Greenwich recast the entire show. You're my understudy now. Bad day to be late."

I lifted my left foot to slide my clog back on, and while I was at it, took a moment to smack Schroeder in the thigh with it. Highly satisfactory.

He rubbed at the spot and scowled at me. "Did you learn nothing in our special bullying assembly?"

"Nothing." I smiled sweetly.

"All right, full cast onstage!" Greenwich hollered. "Let's go, people, we don't have much time!"

I hurried after Schroeder as he moved toward the center aisle, but ended up tripping over a seat that didn't spring back to the upright position. "Ow!" I hobbled the rest of the way out of the row.

"Serves you right," Schroeder whispered with a grin.

I made a face at him, and it was still all twisted up in a trollish expression when someone whispered my name.

Ryan, a stage crew techie, was standing near the side exit with a big black stage light braced against his body.

I rearranged my face into something normal. "*Bonjour, Ry.*" Ryan and I were in the same French class and had been for three years. We always partnered for conversational exercises, because we found each other amusing. Plus, we had about the same skill level—i.e., a false belief that we were much better at French than we probably were.

Ryan beckoned me closer with a jerking head motion. "Listen . . . I was wondering . . . would you want to go to prom with me? As friends." He added the last part quickly, bobbling the light.

"What?" I blinked at him, distracted by concern that he might drop the expensive piece of equipment on his foot.

"I know it's kind of short notice, but I just thought . . ."

"Uhh . . ." If you'd asked me thirty seconds earlier if Ryan was even *thinking* of asking me to prom, I probably would have checked you for fever. Now I had to give him an answer to this out-of-nowhere question? Oh my God, I really did have to answer him. He was staring at me all expectant. "Uhh . . ."

"It's no big deal," he said, shaking his head quickly. "Seriously, just as friends."

"HEART!" Greenwich bellowed. "Onstage. Now."

I winced, and whispered, "Sorry, gotta go!"

"Right. Sorry." Ryan looked away from me and blushed as he backed into the fire bar to shove the techies' entrance open. I leaped toward the stage steps, nearly losing my right clog in my desire to flee. The very definition of smooth. So now I felt like a jerk in addition to being completely clumsy.

"Breakin' hearts, eh, Pancreas?" Schroeder asked as I slid past him to take my place.

My stomach fluttered. "Eavesdrop much?" I raised my eyebrows in an attempt to look indifferent.

"Just observing . . ." Schroeder shrugged.

"What was that?" Lisa whispered.

"Ryan asked me to prom," I whispered back.

Her eyes widened. "Techie Ryan? And you said yes?"

"I didn't say anything, actually."

"All right, people, from the top!" Greenwich shouted. "Try not to be too horrible. I already have a headache."

You'd think a guy whose major accomplishment in life was high school theater would be a little less pretentious.

3 Wherein my brother and I kick Alex Trebek's French-Canadian butt, and I get conscripted as a stunt date

- -

At home, my brother, Phil, was pulling a pizza out of the oven. When it's not football season, Phil is in charge of dinner, which usually translates to pizza, Hamburger Helper, or anything he can transfer directly from the freezer to the microwave.

"*Ooh la la. Très gourmet,*" I teased. I try to work French into my daily life, because I think it adds a certain chicness. Which is totally a word.

Phil laughed through his nose, French style.

"Will Dad be joining us this evening?" I hung my backpack and jacket on the hook by the back door.

"Doubtful." Our dad owns a carpet and flooring company, and no matter how hard he tries, he just never seems to make it home for dinner. The man has an honorary PhD in Leftovers.

"I'll make a salad."

Phil made a gagging sound as he rooted through a drawer for the pizza cutter.

"I'm trying to save you from scurvy, Phil. You should thank me."

"My Flintstones Gummy meets all my anti-scurvy needs, thank you very much."

"Plus, it makes you so mature and classy."

"Just hurry up. It's almost six."

We had a secret, my brother and I. We spent our mealtimes watching *Jeopardy!* and *Wheel of Fortune.* Our grandma used to watch them when she was still alive and babysitting for us every day after school. Now I wasn't sure if it was habit or sentiment, but we were avid fans of Alex and Pat. We could totally win *Jeopardy!* if they let us play as a team.

"Da-da da-da da-da-dah . . ." I sang the theme song to *Jeopardy!* as we settled into our usual spots and Phil took command of the remote. We munched happily for the first round, calling out answers between bites.

At least, I was talking between bites.

Phil had a nasty tendency to talk with his mouth full, so when he said, "Hey, by the way, Amy dumped Troy," it sounded like, "Ay, buyawah, A-E duh Twah."

Luckily, I have a lot of experience talking to my brother around wads of food, so I could answer, "Bummer. He okay?" His friend Troy was one of those football jock types who resembled nothing so much as a teddy bear in shoulder pads. He was super nice. One of Phil's friends that I actually liked. My brother and I were close in age, but we ran in totally different circles.

"Eh." He shrugged and swallowed the last of his pizza. "Anyway, he already had tickets to prom, so I said you'd go with him."

"What?!" He'd said it so casually I almost didn't believe I'd heard him right.

"Come on, it's Troy."

Yeah, sure, I liked Troy, but I had enough prom invitations on my plate as it was. "I can't!"

"Why not?"

"Um, hello? I already planned to go with all my friends, remember?"

"They'll still be there. You can't leave Troy hanging like this."

"How is he possibly my responsibility?" I demanded, twisting on the couch to face my brother.

Phil leaned back and rolled his eyes. "It's not like you have real plans."

"I do, too! Why do you always act like my plans don't count?"

"Don't be such a girl. You're going with a group. It doesn't count."

"For your information, someone asked me to prom just this afternoon."

"Oh." That seemed to stymie him, but only for a moment. "But you just said you were going with your friends."

"Well . . . I didn't tell Ryan yes yet. But that's not the point. The point is, I have two reasons to say no to you pimping me out."

"You didn't say yes? Dude, that's so harsh."

"It wasn't like that." I dismissed him with a wave of my hand. "We got interrupted. It's not like I said no." Conveniently, Ryan had been off in one of the mysterious places techies disappear to when practice ended, so I'd escaped without answering him.

"So you can still say no."

"No!"

"There, see? You just said it. You're good at it."

"Not funny, Phil."

"Do you seriously expect me to tell Troy that he's so pathetic even my little sister won't go to the dance with him? This is going to kill him." Phil grimaced.

"Even if I ignore the fact that you just implied going to the dance with me is pathetic, you are being completely unfair. There's got to be some other girl. Why don't you draft another cheerleader or something? Make Tara scrounge someone up." Tara was my brother's girlfriend.

"Heart. Do this for me. I already told him you would."

"Well, whose fault is that?"

"Come on. You know you want to." This was one of Phil's classic lines. He said it every time he called me for a ride five minutes before curfew.

"I really don't."

"Do it for Troy, then."

"Now you're just playing dirty." I stacked our dishes noisily and stomped toward the kitchen.

"You're going!" Phil called after me.

"I am not!"

"You're going . . . ," he sang out so I'd hear him in the kitchen.

"I'm no-ot!" I sang back. Louder.

4 On the subject of my unappreciated genius

My only option was an emergency three-way call with Cassidy and Lisa.

"Ryan asked you first." Cassidy was firm in her decision from the beginning.

"Technically, Phil said I'd go with Troy first."

"You can't let Phil boss you around like that," Cassidy said.

"You know how he is."

She huffed. "Yeah. Bossy."

"And technically, your friends asked you first," Lisa reminded us. Which they totally did, of course, but since none of my No Drama Prom-a friends had actually *asked* me to prom, it felt, I don't know—rude?—to say no to Ryan and Troy.

"True." I chewed the inside of my cheek. I hate

situations where someone is guaranteed to end up disappointed.

"Oh, come on, we all know that's just the fallback plan," Cassidy said. "The No Drama Prom-a is like your safety school."

"That is so tacky," Lisa said.

"Forget about who asked me first." I needed them to focus. "You have to admit, even though Phil totally should have checked with me, Troy's story is pretty sad."

"Phil shouldn't be involving you at all," Lisa said. "This is not your problem."

"Do you want to go with Troy?" Cassidy wanted to know.

"I don't know, but if Ryan had never asked me, I probably would have said I'd go with Troy. That's got to count for something."

"Except that you already have plans," Lisa interjected.

I ignored Lisa, knowing from years of experience that she would most likely repeat her official stance at every opportunity. "And what if Ryan doesn't just want to go as friends? What if he's, like, trying to segue prom into something more? Doesn't he realize I don't do that sort of thing?"

"Of course he knows. You tell anyone who will listen," Cassidy said.

"But what if he doesn't believe it?"

"Your fear of commitment could not be more cliché," Lisa said.

"It's not fear of commitment!" I protested, like always. I had no fear of commitment. In fact, I really hoped for a committed relationship. Someday. But that day was not until I was a hundred percent certain of my choice of person-I-want-to-spend-the-rest-of-my-life-with, and if there was anything my mother had taught me, it was that eighteen-year-olds were not capable of making that sort of decision. Eighteen-year-olds get knocked up—then do it again when they're nineteen—and then freak out and leave their kids behind for a life of . . . who even knew what my mother was doing? All I'd learned from my grandparents was that she'd always dreamed of being a flight attendant.

Cassidy brought us back to the matter at hand. "Who do you want to go with?"

"I don't know." I shrugged.

"That's the problem. You're too indecisive."

"How is it indecisive not to know? The world is full of mystery."

"Who do you *want* to go with?" Cassidy repeated.

"I . . ." I tried to imagine myself at prom. When I was a little girl, back before I realized that romance was like a field of land mines, I always thought it would be this magical, romantic night where I'd be a princess at my own personal ball, and I'd dance with the love of my life, and stars would shine down on us as we kissed—sweet, puckered up, non-French kisses, because these were my nine-year-old fantasies—during the last song. Now I realize it's just another dance. Don't get me wrong, I've had plenty of good times at dances, but that's all they are. Just a reason to wear a fancy dress and shake your booty to music you wouldn't otherwise be caught dead listening to. The only romance I expected out of prom night was my passionate love for the vintage dress I'd found at Take Two.

"I don't know," I answered in complete honesty.

"Oh, come on," Cassidy groaned. "It's the last dance of the night. A slow song. You're standing in the middle of the dance floor, gazing into the eyes of your prom date. Is it Ryan, or is it Troy?"

I squeezed my eyes shut, trying to put myself in the scene, and God help me if the song from the last scene of that vampire movie wasn't the first music that came to mind. Where was my mental prom taking place—2008? Maybe my middle school self was still in charge of all prom-based fantasies. I could see my hand resting lightly on a shoulder, but when I looked at the face, it was an amorphous blob. Concentrating hard enough to screw up my face, I managed to get the image flickering back and forth between Troy's spiky brownish hair, blue eyes, and wide grin, and Ryan's dark hair, with eyes to match, and his tendency to smile with only half his mouth.

"It could be fun with either of them!" I finally said, with more of an annoying whine than I really like to resort to. I'm fairly certain Brigitte and Audrey never whined.

"You are hopeless," Lisa said. "You should turn them both down and go with the group like you were supposed to."

"I still say whoever asked first wins. That's just good manners," Cassidy said.

"So, Heart, who's it going to be?" Lisa asked.

"I cannot make this decision!"

"You're going to have to eventually." Lisa sighed into the phone, making noisy static for the rest of us. "And you better do it soon, because this topic is already getting tired."

"You're so supportive." They were obviously going to be no help on this.

"Wait!" Cassidy hollered. "I'll ask the Magic 8 Ball!" I could hear her moving on the other end of the line for a minute, then, "Aha! Okay . . . Magic 8 Ball, should Heart go to prom with Ryan?"

"How do we know you're not going to cheat and say whatever you think?" I asked.

"I would never lie about the Magic 8 Ball." Faintly, the sloshing sounds of the toy made their way through the phone. "'Ask again later'? Oh, come on!"

"See? Even the Magic 8 Ball doesn't know what I should do."

Cass ignored that, too. "Should Heart go to prom with Troy?" *Shake, slosh, shake.* "'Concentrate and try again.' You have got to be kidding me."

"I'm telling you, there's no way to make this decision. Even fortune-telling toys won't help me."

Lisa snorted. "Shocking."

"I'll ask it again later and report back to you tomorrow," Cassidy said.

"If you must." I draped myself across my bed with one hand against my forehead. Sometimes I think those silent film stars had it right. Melodrama can be so cathartic.

"Trust me. It's in the hands of fate."

I let my tongue loll out like I was dying from her poisonous words. Fate is only a comfort if you actually believe in it.

5 Concerning the questionable fortune-telling powers of toys

- -

Cassidy and I have our first class together, so I suspected she'd have a full report on the Magic 8 Ball experiments as soon as I walked in. I was right.

"Okay, this is downright bizarre." She waved a piece of paper at me. "I asked the Ball twenty times about Ryan and twenty about Troy, and look at this." Flattening the paper on her desktop, she pointed to a chart. "It's, like, completely equal."

She'd written down each response in two neat columns. They were even color-coded with red, green, and yellow dots next to each answer.

"You have too much time on your hands," I said.

"It was fascinating!" she insisted. "See? Greens are yeses, reds are nos, and yellows are those annoying unhelpful answers."

Scanning the sheet, I saw that she was right. There were seven greens in each column, eight yellows, and five reds. "Wow, that is kind of weird."

"I'm telling you. We might need to consult another source."

I raised my eyebrow. "Don't say a Ouija board."

"Please." She rolled her eyes. "Tarot cards and your horoscope."

Before I could reply, Schroeder's voice startled us both. "Did I miss some major assignment?" And then, before I could stop him, he was looking over Cassidy's shoulder at her chart. "What is that?"

"Never mind." I snatched the sheet and shoved it into the pocket of my dress. Schroeder was the last person I wanted to see the chart. I knew without a doubt he'd tease me, and I didn't need that today. Besides, he was in the No Drama Prom-a Crew, so I was technically about to ditch him. I doubted everyone would be as enthusiastic about my last-minute change of plans as Cassidy.

"Heart's got two invitations to the prom, and we're trying to figure out who she should go with," Cassidy answered his question.

I closed my eyes for a second, fighting the urge to stomp on her foot. Maybe I'd spend my first class drafting an ad for a new best friend.

"I thought we were going together. All of us, I mean."
Schroeder's eyes narrowed.

"I was . . . am . . . might be." I sighed.

He laid a hand over his chest. "Heart, I'm wounded.
You're ditching us?"

And now I felt guilty. Wonderful. "It's complicated."

"Not really, Ditcher." He grinned, but didn't look very
amused.

"It's not like that." I scowled at him, but his grin didn't
fade. He just shook his head and sighed.

"No, I see how it is. You don't want to go with me.
With any of us." He sighed again. "And we were going to
have such a great time. Bad food, terrible music, watching
the cheerleaders hold each other's hair back after too much
Boone's Farm wine . . ." Another sigh.

I raised my eyebrow. "Wow, you really know how to
sell a girl."

"What can I say?" He shrugged.

"So, who do you think she should go with?" Cassidy asked. "Ryan from stage crew, or her brother's friend
Troy?"

Schroeder's eyebrows pulled together momentarily.
"Ryan asked you?"

My cheeks went hot. "Yeah."

"Are you going with him?"

"I don't know. I can't figure out what to do."

"And who's Troy again?"

I waved a hand. "My brother's friend. It's a pity date. His girlfriend dumped him."

"So, which one would you go with?" Cassidy asked him.

He appeared to be considering her question for a moment, before slowly looking at me, then back to Cassidy. "Neither."

"Very helpful."

"Wasn't trying to be." He turned on his heel and went down the aisle toward his seat.

"Clearly, this is an impossible decision," I said.

"After class, I'm checking your horoscope."

6 On the superiority of the cafeteria's french fries and near-death experiences at the hands of said fries

I don't know what it was about the school cafeteria's french fries, but they were my drug of choice, and I had no interest in twelve-stepping my way out of this addiction. So I was completely lost in french fry anticipation when a touch at my elbow made me jump. I turned, heart pounding, to find Troy Rafferty smiling at me. Except it was not a real smile. Sure, his lips were shoved into approximately the right position, but his eyes hadn't gotten the memo. He looked like a sad clown with a smiling mouth painted on. It bordered on creepy. "Hey, Heart."

"Troy!" I clapped my dollar bill to my chest. "You scared me."

"Look, I know your brother told you about Amy."

"Yeah, sorry." I squinched up my face, not sure if this was a full-on hugging moment or not. I settled for a quick pat on the shoulder.

"So, I know it's short notice and all, but if you wanted to come to prom with me, that would be pretty cool."

And the nominees for least enthusiastic prom invitation are . . .

"Oh, um." It was a lot harder to say no to Troy himself rather than Phil, who as the messenger, deserved whatever punishment I could dream up. Troy was the guy who always made sure to say hello to me when Phil's friends were over, and he'd even given me a ride home from school once or twice when Phil was busy. A genuinely good human being.

"If you don't want to, that's cool." Troy looked down, and I swear to God, I thought he was going to start crying. Ginormous, six-foot-four, two-hundred-and-fifty-pound Troy Rafferty was going to break down in the french fry line.

Damn you, Amy.

"It's not that." I jiggled my hands in front of me, hoping to somehow stem the potential tide of tears. "It's just that someone else asked me and—"

"That's cool," Troy said softly. "Sorry to bother you." He started to lumber away, and my heart crumpled.

"Troy, wait!" I put a hand on his back. "Uh . . . let me talk to . . . him. The other guy, I mean. I'll, like, let you know, okay?"

A miniature sunrise of relief warmed his face, making his blue eyes look happy for the first time. He smiled and nodded. "Yeah, okay. That'd be great."

Well, that settled it. I'd just have to tell Ryan I couldn't go. Clearly, Troy was a man in need. Besides, this way Phil wouldn't be pissed at me, and I am all about maximizing the number of people I can keep happy at any given time, especially people in my family. And at least I didn't have to worry that Troy was expecting anything to happen between us after the dance. More importantly, how could I possibly say no to someone who was on the verge of tears?

Then, of course, because I was having the kind of day that is normally only found in teen movies from the 1990s, I ran into Ryan almost immediately after paying for my fries.

"Heart!"

"Ryan . . ." I tried to force some enthusiasm, but ended up making a weird warbling sound at the end. I wrinkled my nose, hoping he hadn't noticed.

"Um, listen . . . about the prom . . ." He looked around and touched my arm. "Do you have a minute?"

Honest to God, my first thought was: He's going to uninvite me—hallelujah! Luckily, I managed to keep my reply to a more polite, "Sure."

Ryan led me, and my french fries, to a remote corner

table where no one sat—probably because its vicinity to the recycling bins made the floor permanently sticky. I found a relatively clean spot to stand and popped a fry in my mouth. No sense letting them get cold.

"So . . . we're friends, right?"

I gave him a confused look. "Yeah, of course. We've bonded over French, Ryan. That's not the sort of thing I take lightly."

He smiled and laughed nervously. "I just feel like I should be honest with you," he said. "I didn't want you to think that I was asking you because . . . that we . . . that I . . ." He took a frustrated breath and let it out in a short huff. "I'm gay."

My tongue went psychotic, and the fry lodged in my throat. I wheezed as my lungs reacted to the sudden loss of fresh air. Eyes bugging and filling with tears simultaneously, I let out a cough that sent the fry out of my mouth like a bullet. It splatted on the floor right beside the Aluminum Cans bin while I sputtered and coughed some more and tried not to vomit. Ryan thumped me on the back a couple of times until I finally got a deep breath. I grasped his arm for support, panting for a second, then finally managed to croak, "What?"

"Oh my God. Are you all right?"

"Yeah," I coughed. "I'm sorry, I just choked a little." I patted my throat. "You were saying?"

He laughed nervously. "I'm, uh . . . gay."

I nodded enthusiastically, trying to smile even though my eyes were still watering. "That's what I thought you said."

"Before you choked."

"I absolutely promise you the choking was not about what you said."

"Really?" He looked doubtful. "Because it pretty much seemed like a cause-effect kind of thing."

"Okay, it might have been a little bit about what you said, but not in a bad way, I swear." I used a knuckle to wipe below my eyes.

"You're sure?"

"Completely."

"Because it was kind of like the worst thing I could imagine after coming out to someone for the first time."

Thank God I had the foresight not to put another fry in my mouth, because I swear I almost choked again. "The first time?"

He laughed again, nervous. "Um . . . yeah."

"*Mon dieu!* I'm . . . I'm honored!" I threw my free hand around his neck, hugging him as best as I could with my muscles still feeling like jelly after nearly dying, and a container of fries in my other hand.

Ryan made a strange sound, somewhere between a laugh and a sob. "Thank you."

"So no one else knows? Your parents?"

"I think my mom suspects, but I haven't said anything."

The weight of being the first person he'd told was intense. To think of all the years we'd been friends, and I'd never even had a clue. Malfunctioning gaydar, for sure. "Why me?"

He shrugged. "You're just . . . you're really nice. And I know you don't really date anyone from school, so I thought . . . I don't know exactly. I just needed to finally tell someone. And I guess I figured you wouldn't tell anyone. I don't want this getting around right now."

"Well, thank you. I guess." Was that the right thing to say?

"So, about prom—?"

"Oh." I was surprised he was back to that so quickly after dropping such a huge piece of news on me.

"The thing is, I didn't want you to think that I, like, liked you and be weirded out by that or anything."

I laughed, as if that was the furthest thing from my mind. Silly Ryan, why on earth would I make such psycho assumptions? Perish the thought!

Ryan went on, "I just wanted to go and have fun with someone who wouldn't make a big deal out of it."

I felt strangely important, but all I could think to do was nod.

"So, you'll go? Even though it's not going to be some big romantic night for you?"

I rolled my eyes. "Please. There is zero possibility for romance among any of my potential dates for this gig."

His face fell. "There's a lot?"

Stupid. "No, I mean, well, I was supposed to go with a big group. You know, Cassidy, and Ally, and Kim, and Schroeder, and Dan, and Pat, and Neel." I bobbed my head along with the list.

"Oh." His disappointment was palpable.

"But that wasn't, like, set in stone or anything." Apart from the fact that I already paid for my ticket, and signed up for a table of eight with the rest of the crew.

"Oh," he said again, this time with hope.

And then I remembered Troy. Damn it. I had just talked to the guy, for heaven's sake. What was wrong with me? I didn't remember anyone getting amnesia from a near-death french fry experience on any of my grandma's soap operas. "Let me talk to them. Is that . . .

you don't mind, do you?"

"No." He shook his head. "But can you not tell them about me?"

"Of course! I wouldn't!"

"Okay. Then, yeah. Just let me know later, okay?"

"Great." *Procrastination, thy name is Heart LaCoeur.* "Um, thanks again. For telling me, I mean."

"Thanks for not actually choking to death from the shock."

I laughed. "Hey, you know, we're French buddies, we go way back."

"*Les amis français,*" he corrected with one finger raised.

"*Ah, bien sûr.*"

"I'll see you at rehearsal later." He waved a little and backed away a few steps before heading for his usual seat.

Oh man, I was in trouble now.

7 Wherein the deities desert me, and I give myself over to the power of statistics

----

I had a feeling I'd already exhausted my friends' patience on the who-should-Heart-go-to-the-prom-with front, and I couldn't tell them the secret Ryan had entrusted me with, so I was stuck mulling over the decision on my own for the rest of the day. Cassidy's idiotic Magic 8 Ball chart wasn't getting any more helpful stuffed into my pocket, and so far no signs had come down from the heavens to clue me in. Not that I seriously expected one, of course, but part of me was hoping, I have to admit. Any deity would be welcome as long as he or she came equipped with an answer.

If only my mother had named me Heaven instead of Heart . . .

No, scratch that.

I was no closer to a decision when I slipped into chem

class and climbed onto my designated stool at the lab table I shared with Schroeder.

"'Sup, Duodenum?" he said with a slight tilt of his mouth.

"Schroeder." I looked down my nose at him. Even though I was impressed by his seemingly endless knowledge of internal organs, I had to keep up the illusion that he was successfully annoying me.

He took forever settling into his seat, dropping his bag and shrugging out of his hooded sweatshirt. It was always hot in the labs. Underneath his sweatshirt he was wearing the dark green shirt we'd gotten for being in the fall play last year. Either he'd grown or the shirt had shrunk since last year, because it was much tighter around his biceps than I remembered. It's not like I go around cataloging the fit of Schroeder's wardrobe, but he has really nice forearms, so I could hardly help myself. It's probably from all the piano playing.

"Listen," he said in a soft voice, pulling my attention back to his face. "I was thinking I could get my little sister to make one of those fortune-teller things if you still haven't made up your mind about prom." Schroeder held up both hands, pinched his fingers and thumbs together, and made them move like the paper toy he alluded to.

"Remind me to thank Cassidy for being such a big mouth." She must have told him the whole Magic 8 Ball story.

He laughed. "She also told me it was her idea, if that makes any difference."

"Minor."

"So, have you come to your senses yet? Coming with the No Drama Prom-a as planned?" He lifted his eyebrows expectantly.

"Oh." I twisted my mouth.

"You're not, are you?" He sounded disappointed. And not in a fake aww-what-a-shame way, but more like a Heart-I'm-very-disappointed-in-your-behavior way.

With a sigh, I lowered my head to the lab table's surface and wove my fingers together behind my neck. "Maybe I shouldn't go at all."

"You can't do that," he said quickly.

"Why not?" I asked the cold table.

"Because . . ." He paused, long enough to make me sneak a peek at him through the fringe of my hair. "Then you're letting the drama win!" He said it like it'd just come to him, and I turned my head far enough to cast a raised eyebrow in his direction. "You can't let the prom win."

I laughed. "The prom is out to get me?" It probably was. That would just figure.

"I'm just saying, if you don't go at all, you'll only sit at home obsessing about it."

"I would not obsess. It's a stupid dance."

"So . . ." He drew an elaborate, invisible design with his finger on the lab table. "Just pick someone and be done with it."

"It's not that easy."

The bell rang, and our teacher was instantly at the board with a squeaky marker and a passion for radioactive isotopes.

Schroeder leaned close, his voice low enough to escape detection but loud enough to let his irritation be heard. "You're overthinking it. Flip a coin or something. Heads you go with us, tails you still go with us."

He was joking, obviously, but there was a certain logic to it. My father used to pull a similar trick when we were growing up. If we couldn't decide between ice-cream flavors or something like that, he'd stick two small objects behind his back and make us pick a hand. I can still hear him saying, *The penny is chocolate; the nickel is bubble gum. Pick one.* The best part was, if you picked one and you got that awful pang of regret, you knew you actually wanted the other kind more. It was simple. Almost elegant.

I'd just make Troy heads and Ryan tails and flip for it. I'd know if I made the right decision as soon as I saw the result, wouldn't I? I tapped my pen against my notebook, wondering if this was too simplistic.

Still . . . at least I'd know how I felt. And no one would have to know. I could do it right now. It didn't have to be some huge Super Bowl coin toss, after all. Just a simple flick of my thumb and I could have this whole problem solved.

That's it. I was doing it. I patted my pockets and came up empty. Shoot.

I leaned over to Schroeder and whispered, "Got a quarter?"

He tilted away from me first, checking his right pocket, then switched to check the left, knocking his head against mine. "Sorry!" he whispered. "You okay?"

I rubbed my temple, tempted to give him a sour look, but stifling the urge since he was doing me a favor. So I smiled and nodded instead. The muffled jingling of coins was unmistakable, and in a moment, he emerged with a few coins.

"No quarters," he said. "But I can get you a game of skee-ball at Chuck E. Cheese." He pointed to a gold token in his palm.

I laughed, pressing my fingers to my lips so I wouldn't be too loud. "Why do you have a token for Chuck E. Cheese?"

He gave me a don't-be-so-judgmental look. "It was my cousin's birthday over the weekend."

I took the token from his cupped hand, noticing how warm his skin was without being sweaty. A rare trait in a boy. "Thanks."

"They don't work in the vending machine, trust me," he said softly, nudging a dime out of the pile with a fingertip.

"This is all I need, thanks. I'll give it right back."

He shot me a confused look, which melted the instant he saw me fit the coin against my bent thumb. "You can't flip a coin over this," he hissed.

"Why not?"

"Do you really think fate is going to guide you or something?"

"I don't believe in fate. This is pure statistics."

"So, what is it? Chuck E.'s head you come with us, tails you go with one of them?"

"Nope." I waited until Mr. Lenier turned to write on the board again and flicked my thumb, sending the coin up.

Tokens are lighter than quarters, as it turns out, and

the thing flew up in the air almost to the ceiling. I gasped as it clattered once—too loudly—against the edge of the lab desk before falling to points unknown.

Mr. Lenier turned around, looking for the source of the noise, but Schroeder and I kept our best poker faces on and he went back to his radioactive decay.

After a moment of watching Lenier's back, I whispered, "Where'd it go?" and searched around the bottom of my stool. Schroeder did the same, twisting and tilting, and nearly knocking heads with me a couple more times. Finally, I caught a flash of something gold a few feet away, near the wall. "There." I pointed.

"You are not seriously doing this," he hissed.

"Why not?" I asked, leaning out as far as I could without leaving my seat. Damn, I still couldn't see which side of the coin was up. "It's as good as any other way of deciding."

"This isn't like picking which movie to see. These are human beings."

"It's not like they have to know about it. Besides, it's just a dumb coin toss. It doesn't actually control my fate."

He narrowed his eyes. "All right then. What's it say?"

PART 2

and the
winner is . . .

Prom Night

8 In which I am thoroughly humiliated by someone who isn't even there, and ponder the mysteries of alcohol procurement

- -

HEADS

The major drawback of going to prom with Troy was the fact that I couldn't go to Ally's house to get ready with the rest of my friends. The logistics were too annoying. So it was just me and my brother, who, of course, had no idea about the intricacies of formal dance preparation. I might not be in this for the romance, but I was definitely going to live it up in the glamour department.

My hair took me three hours to set, but I was determined to have a full head of pin curls. The job was shoulder-breaking labor, and I almost decided to scrap the whole thing a few times. I couldn't let my true date for the prom down, though—my gorgeous, frothy lavender dress. It was from the fifties or sixties—Lucille at Take Two hadn't been completely sure—and it was a girly dream.

Layers of sheer material made the skirt flounce out, and the sweetheart bodice was crazy flattering. It fit perfectly—I so love the way vintage clothes are made for people who actually have some curves—I felt like a total bombshell. Maybe Brigitte was the name for me, after all. Or Marilyn. Ooh! That one was going on the list.

When at last I sailed down the stairs to show myself to Phil, I did my best Marilyn Monroe pout/head tilt and said in her trademark breathy voice, "Well? How do I look?"

Phil, already in his tux, and playing some video game that seemed to involve killing a lot of South American drug lords, barely glanced up. "Fine."

Talk about a letdown. I collapsed from my Marilyn pose and sighed. "Great, thanks."

"What?"

"I put a lot of work into this outfit. You could at least fake being interested."

"But then you'd know I was faking."

"I'd rather you fake it than give me 'Fine.'"

With an exaggerated sigh, he paused his game and turned to look at me. "You're wearing an old dress to prom?"

"It's vintage!" I protested.

"Whatever. Look weird if you want to."

I stepped up to the couch and grabbed one of the loose pillows from the end to swat him in the head.

"Hey! Watch it!" Phil was a brunette, like me—well beyond average brown, and into the chestnut range—but he treated his hair about the same as most guys I knew. In other words, what couldn't be handled by shampoo could be handled by a hat. Even though he'd showered and applied some kind of product to it, I could make out the faint indentation in the back where his cap always rested.

"When are they supposed to get here?" I peeked through the living room window, but there was no sign of a limo. Phil and his friends were going all out with the prom stereotypes. They had a limo for the whole night, and I'd heard a rumor that one of the guys had a hotel room.

"Dunno. Soon."

Such a helper, my brother.

A glint of sun at the end of the block pulled my attention to a car approaching, but the shape was way too boxy to be the limo, and after a second, I could tell it was my dad's truck. "The prodigal father returneth," I announced.

"All right, Pop." Phil laughed. "What was the

over-under on the clock?"

I grinned. Sometimes Phil and I made bets on when our dad would get home.

The big white van rolled into the driveway and lurched to a stop. LACOEUR CARPET AND FLOORING, the painted sign on the side read. WHERE THE HEART IS. Oh, how I hate that slogan. It's a play on our last name, and it had been the slogan since my grandpa started the company, but when your only daughter just happens to have the first name Heart, you'd think a guy would have the decency not to doom her to an implied imprisonment in a carpet warehouse.

Our dad got out and hitched up the back of his pants as he ambled toward the door.

"Five bucks says he doesn't remember it's prom tonight," I said.

"You're on." Phil powered off the video game console and stood to wait with me.

"'Lo?" Dad called as he came in through the kitchen.

"Hey, Pops," Phil hollered in return.

When he appeared in the doorway that led from the kitchen to the hall, I was struck suddenly by how big he was. A monster of a guy—six-three, somewhere in the neighborhood of 225 on the scale, though he seemed to carry it all in his shoulders. A lifetime of manual labor will do that to you, I guess. That and turn your knees into rusty hinges. He did a double take when he spotted me, and I was certain I'd bagged Phil's five bucks.

"Look at you, sweetheart." The fatigue slipped from his face and he smiled softly, blue eyes suddenly blurred through potential tears. "You're so beautiful."

"Dad." I tried to dismiss the compliment, but inside I was filled to the brim with sudden warmth.

"I was worried I wouldn't make it in time to see you before the dance," Dad said.

I got a poke in the back from Phil. I owed him five bucks, after all. "We're still here."

"You guys look great." Dad approached with his arms extended, but hesitated before touching me. "It okay for me to hug you, or am I gonna wrinkle you?"

I laughed and stepped into his embrace. "It's okay, Daddy." My father was many things—perpetually late, nearly always tired when he arrived, and a proud blue-collar guy who liked beer and NASCAR and was totally mystified by Broadway—but I never had to wonder if he loved us.

"So, you're all set for tonight?"

"We're good, Pop." Phil clapped him on the shoulder.

"You sure? You need money or anything?"

"Well, if you're offering . . ." Phil put on a fake bashful smile and held out his hand.

"You." Dad rolled his eyes and knocked it away. "I'm more worried about my little girl getting home safe."

"I'll be fine, Dad. Everybody's spending the night at Neel's, remember? I can get a ride home from someone in the morning." I didn't know what the after-prom plans were for Phil and his friends, but as long as they didn't involve crossing any international borders, I was pretty sure I'd make it to Neel's house without any trouble. If I knew my brother at all, there would be a party and beer involved. It would be easy to slip away after the official prom part was over and hitch a ride with one of my friends straight from the dance. No problem.

"I almost forgot. Colleen stopped by today. She wanted me to give you guys something. I think I left it in the truck. Hang on." As our father lumbered toward the back door again, Phil and I exchanged wary glances. Our aunt Colleen had long seen herself as the substitute mom we never asked for after our own left. She was one of those women who referred to herself as "forty-five and fabulous" and swore up and down that we could ask her anything—"And I mean *anything*." Well-meaning, but inevitably embarrassing, the idea that she'd prepared something special for Phil and me on prom night was nothing short of terrifying.

Luckily, at that moment, a strange bleating version of "Look Away, Dixieland" caught our attention from down the street. It repeated, getting louder. I stepped back to peek through the living room windows. The limo had arrived, and the horn was most definitely of the novelty variety.

"Hallelujah. Let's get out of here before Dad finds Colleen's care packages," I said, grabbing Phil by the wrist.

"Right in front of you." Phil put on some speed, grabbing the clear corsage box for his girlfriend from the front hall, yanking open the front door, and pulling me by the wrist down the three steps to the sidewalk before the limo was even stopped in front of the house. "Our ride's here, Dad!" he hollered, as if our father would somehow miss the merrily caroling stretch SUV limo cruising to a halt at our curb.

"Just a sec!" Dad emerged from the truck once again, this time brandishing two small cellophane bags. The kind you get when you go to a kid's birthday party when you're little. These particular ones were clear pink and decorated with hearts.

"You have *got* to be kidding me," I muttered.

"If we break for the car, he'll never catch us. His knees

can't take it." Phil looked at the limo with a calculating eye.

The black limo finally came to a stop with a loud *AAAOOOOGAH!* blast from the horn. Oh good, I thought, novelty with options. Phil's friend Doug burst up through the sunroof, howling his own version of the horn. "Let's get this party started!" he bellowed.

Phil made some kind of wolf howl of his own, and for the first time, butterflies flapped their wings in my stomach. I was about to go to prom with a bunch of jocks and their girlfriends. This was not my crowd. This wasn't even my species. What had I gotten myself into?

The back door opened, and I caught a glimpse of brightly colored dresses and a whole lot of legs before my view was completely obscured by Troy, hauling himself from the depths of the backseat.

"What's up, you guys?" He grinned, his face pink. "Heart, you look really pretty."

"Thanks."

"Here." My dad's big hand thrust into view, holding out the treat bag. "From Colleen."

"Dad . . . ," I protested weakly. "Can you put it in the house for me?"

"She said you'd need this stuff."

"Firecrackers and whiskey?" Phil said hopefully, taking the little Baggie and shaking it.

"What?" Troy was watching the whole exchange with unfocused eyes, and it occurred to me that he might have been drinking. I wasn't surprised, per se, but it did seem a little early for bleary-eyed confusion. The sun was still up, for heaven's sake.

"Oh, wait—I have a corsage for you, Heart." He looked back toward the limo, as if wondering how the flowers had escaped him.

"Never mind. We gotta get going." Phil tossed the bag from Colleen to Dad without another glance. "I don't need this, Pop."

Our dad was at a loss, holding Phil's care package. I didn't have the heart to make him take mine back, too. Colleen might be a real pain sometimes, but she was family, and I didn't want to hurt her feelings, even if she'd never find out about it. Unfortunately, I had no convenient place to stash my goodie bag. My small beaded clutch purse was just big enough for my phone, the vintage cigarette case I used as a wallet, and my lip gloss. Apparently, designers from the past didn't realize cell phones would be taking up prime purse real estate. Imagine.

"Aren't I supposed to take pictures or something?"

Dad patted his pockets, like he expected to find a camera miraculously waiting in one of them. A tape measure was a much more likely candidate.

"We're doing that at Tara's house." Phil's girlfriend was our last scheduled pickup for the night.

"Oh. Okay." Dad tucked his thumbs through his belt loops and shrugged. "I guess you should go then."

I darted in to give him another quick hug. "We'll show you pictures tomorrow."

"Have fun tonight, sweetheart." He gave me a rough kiss on the temple. "Call me if you need me to come get you or anything."

I rolled my eyes but patted him on the shoulder. "Dad, I won't get into trouble, okay?"

"Let's go!" a female voice called from inside.

Phil thwacked me in the back with his hand. "Come on, Heart."

Wiggling my fingers at my dad, I followed Phil into the depths of the limo.

What followed could have been filmed by National Geographic for a special on the Mating Rituals of the American Jock. A bunch of guttural grunting, high fives, and ass slapping from the males in the car, squealing and giggling from the girls accompanied by some flirtatious adjusting of their brightly colored dresses, which might as well have been exotic feathers on birds. Someone passed Phil a flask before the door was even closed, which he passed to me as Troy wedged himself into a seat.

"What is this?" I asked.

"Who cares?" One of the girls, Randi, laughed.

I sniffed at the neck of the flask and tried not to wince when my eyes started watering.

"Bottoms up!" Troy grinned.

I pressed it against my lips and tipped it back, but didn't let any of the liquid into my mouth. Still, my tongue burned when I licked my lips afterward. I grimaced for effect and passed the flask to Troy.

"Take it easy, lightweight," Phil said. He knew I didn't run with a drinking crowd. Not up to the level of Phil and his friends, anyway. Of course, there are probably Russians in rehab who couldn't outdrink Phil and his friends. At least with the limo, I knew I wasn't going to get the call to come pick my brother up at some godforsaken hour of the night because he was too drunk to drive. Not that I'd had to do that a few dozen times or anything.

"I'm fine," I told him.

Troy took a pull from the neck and passed it on before handing me an oddly geometric plastic box with a corsage inside. It was made up of several orange flowers with black ribbons—our school colors—and a small plastic charm dangling from the middle of the bow, like something you'd see on a kid's birthday cake. I flipped the white disk over to see a snarling tiger's face.

"Cool, huh?" Troy asked. "I didn't know they had mascot stuff."

I smiled weakly. "Me either." A tiger? He got me a plastic tiger to put around my wrist? I hated to be ungrateful, but come *on*. "Thanks."

"You're welcome. Go Tigers, right?" He beamed. He actually beamed. It was adorably clueless.

I slipped it over my wrist, sneaking a look at the other girls' flowers. I was the only one with a school-spirit-themed monstrosity. I pressed my lips together to stifle a laugh. Maybe that was the risk a girl took going to prom with a big oaf like Troy. At least he was a lovable oaf.

The limo took a right turn, sending us all wobbling in our seats. As I shifted to regain my balance, my little cellophane treat bag from Aunt Colleen fell to the floor.

"Ooh, there's gum in there!" Randi snatched it off the floor before I could reach it. "I forgot to bring mine." She opened the twist tie and spilled the contents onto the short, fluffy skirt of her tangerine-colored dress.

"Whoa! What's this?" Phil's asshole friend Doug pinched something from the tangle on Randi's lap and held it up for everyone to see. A strip of three condoms. "Damn, Phil, your sister's a bad girl!" He cackled.

I am a hard person to embarrass. I mean, sure, my ears heat up if I trip in front of a group of people, but never for more than a second. It comes from years of being in plays, I think. When you have to take your clothes off as fast as possible with a group of other people for a quick costume change, there is no time for modesty. Plus, if you really think about it, being in a play is essentially playing pretend in front of an audience. You gotta have some guts to make that not humiliating, right?

But when Doug started waving the short strip of condoms like a victory flag, I pretty much wanted to die. This was the exact opposite of the reputation I'd worked so hard to cultivate over the last three years. Now I was not only the girl who was available at the last minute to be Troy's date, I was the girl who obviously intended to sleep with Troy. Three times.

This moment of abject humiliation brought to you by Aunt Colleen. Aunt Colleen, when your average embarrassment just won't do.

"Those aren't mine," I croaked, but no one really heard me over the laughter and hooting.

"God! Are you, like, twelve?" Randi grabbed the condoms from Doug's hand. "Don't be so immature."

"What?" Doug protested.

Randi rolled her eyes and held the condoms out to me. "Here, Heart, put these away so you don't offend the children."

"Thank you," I said softly, shoving them into my tiny clutch purse. I didn't want the damn things, but I couldn't think of a better way to get them out of sight.

I tried to catch Phil's eye across the limo, but he was too busy laughing at something someone else had said. The flask had made its way around to him again, and he tipped it back, then made a face as nothing came out. He made a show of turning it upside down over the floor, letting only a single droplet of clear liquid fall.

"Next!" Troy announced. He reached inside his tuxedo jacket and emerged with a small glass bottle of brown liquid. After taking the first drink, he offered it to me. "Here you go."

I did another of my fake sips before handing it off to Randi, who still had the rest of Aunt Colleen's care package spilled on her lap. Trying not to look obvious, I skimmed my eyes over the remaining stuff. Randi had taken the gum, leaving a cherry lip gloss, a quarter and a dime—did she seriously think I'd be using a pay phone tonight?—a small roll of Rolaids, a hair holder and some bobby pins, a book of matches, and three bandages. Grudgingly, I had to admit that some of it seemed potentially useful. Though what she thought I was going to do with matches eluded me—was there some kind of campfire tradition I wasn't aware of? I tapped Randi on the shoulder and pointed to her lap. She made a go-ahead gesture, and I started tucking everything into my clutch. By the time I'd squirreled it all away, the clasp would barely close, and the whole thing looked like an overcooked sausage.

Suddenly, the limo banked toward the curb, and I realized we were at Tara's house. A bunch of adults were out on the lawn, cameras snapping away as the limo rolled to a stop, and a second later, Tara herself emerged from the house.

She looked gorgeous, as my brother's girlfriend was prone to do. Tara was everything high school girls are told we should want to be: just the right height, slim, blond, white-toothed, and blue-eyed. It was like she was built in a factory. Tonight, her hair was a perfect tumble of waves, and her dress was somewhere between silver and white. It was impossible to tell by the way it sparkled in the evening sunlight.

Phil looked suddenly more handsome when he hopped

out to greet her. She accepted the white-and-silver, and noticeably tiger-free, wrist corsage he'd been holding since we left the house, and a kiss on the cheek. Then her parents were waving everyone out of the limo for the obligatory prom photographs. I realized the adults on the lawn were the parents of some of the other kids from the limo when they started calling to their children and asking for individual portraits and so on. Biting my lip, I looked at Phil. Were we supposed to tell Dad to come over? Was he the only parent not here playing amateur paparazzi? Why did everyone seem to know prom secrets that I'd somehow missed?

This time, Phil actually felt me staring at him. I nodded toward the other parents and made a face I hoped said, "Did we screw up?" Phil just rolled his eyes. But I still felt guilty. Dad probably would have liked to be here.

Someone grabbed my elbow and dragged me toward the line of girls arranged on the lawn. There were only four of us, but I was clearly the odd one out. Sparkly Tara, poufy tangerine-colored Randi, and Olivia in sequined, pageant-ready teal. Then there was me, in my vintage lavender. Not to mention the fact that I was the shortest, and the only one who appeared to eat on a regular basis.

I swallowed hard, wishing there had been a decent way

to get out of this pity date without hurting Troy and disappointing my brother. If I were with my friends, I wouldn't be the only one not dressed in the latest Nordstrom's prom offerings. I knew for a fact that Cassidy was wearing sparkly pink Chuck Taylors, for example.

"Come by me, Heart!" Tara beckoned me with an outstretched hand. She meant well, I knew, but I felt like such the afterthought little sister as I took her hand and let her pull me between herself and Olivia.

The moms bossed us around for a while into a series of poses with and without the boys. Then it was individual couples' photos, and I found myself standing with Troy's hot hand on my waist. It was a gorgeous evening, in the seventies and clear, but in his tuxedo, Troy was baking. He already had a sheen of sweat on his forehead, which was probably just as well since it helped disguise the blush of alcohol in his cheeks and nose.

Eventually, we were released, and we all climbed back into the limo. It was crowded in there now, and I ended up with part of my skirt under Troy's leg, making it impossible to move. More bottles of alcohol were produced, going around and around the group. I don't know where they'd been hiding it all, or how they'd gotten their hands on so much. It was baffling. The speed of drinking increased as the landmarks indicated we were approaching the dance. Despite my efforts to only fake sipping, a few bumps in the road sent a couple of swigs into my mouth, and I tried not to choke on the taste of pure alcohol. It wasn't that I'd never had a drink before, but I'd never taken shots straight from the bottle. And definitely never from bottles that had been secured against warm bodies. Vodka burns so much harder when it's a cozy 98.6 degrees.

Then, at last, our limo made it to the drop-off point, and we climbed down onto the sidewalk.

"Let's prom it up!" Doug shouted, raising a fist in victory.

"Thanks again for coming with me," Troy said, giving me a sappy look. He used his sleeve to blot sweat away from his hairline, but his sleeve wasn't going to do anything for his boozy breath.

"Sure! It'll be fun!" I said, because apparently I'm insane.

9   Wherein Ryan's trusty steed proves
    completely untrustworthy, and I am
    almost kidnapped by a psychotic
    serial killer

TAILS

My dad is surprisingly technology-savvy, considering he sells and installs carpet for a living. That does not, however, mean he has any skill as a photographer, despite owning a decent digital camera. So pictures with Ryan took longer than I expected. He kept checking the LCD screen for how the shots turned out, and he was never satisfied. By the end, I had a cramp in my lower back from standing in the same pose for so long.

It was a relief to sink into the passenger seat of Ryan's old Jeep.

"What's in the package?" Ryan asked, indicating the cellophane treat bag my dad had handed me at the last minute.

"Something from my crazy aunt Colleen," I sighed.

"Crazy, like, there's going to be a lock of human hair in that bag?"

I burst into laughter. "No, not that kind of crazy. More like she wants to be my surrogate mom. Unfortunately, she wants to be one of those 'cool' moms who says I can talk to her about anything."

Ryan grinned. "So what's in the bag?"

"Let's find out."

Ryan lifted the gearshift back into park and turned to watch me open it with interest.

I named each thing as I pulled it out. "Rolaids . . . gum . . . bobby pins . . . ," then choked as I pulled out a strip of three condoms. Laughing, I waved them at Ryan. "Oh, baby, we'll be putting these to some good use later!"

"You really think three's enough?" He looked thoughtful. "We can swing by Walgreens and pick up a jumbo pack."

Giggling, I turned over the condoms to read the packaging. "'Pleasure shaped'! What the heck does that mean?"

"You're asking me?" Ryan shifted the car into drive and headed into the street.

"Colleen is so clueless." I shook my head.

"I don't know. It could be worse."

"How?"

"She could have stuffed a chastity belt in there."

I grinned. "Maybe just a statuette of Jesus and some pamphlets about abstinence."

Ryan snorted. "That's more like what *my* aunt would give me."

"Yikes."

"Yeah," he drawled. "You can imagine I'm not real excited about coming out to the extended family."

I looked down at my lap, uncomfortable suddenly. I couldn't imagine what it would be like knowing someone in your family might hate you for who you are. "What about your parents?"

"My mom will be fine. My dad . . . I don't know. I think he'll be kind of shocked, but we should be okay."

"Hmm." I honestly didn't know what to say to that. Is there sage advice to be given to people who could be risking disownership from their families? It made me sick to think that was even a possibility. I looked down at the orange tiger lily in the corsage Ryan had brought me, and fiddled with the yellow ribbon tied below it. Somehow, he'd managed to find a corsage that didn't come with a wrist strap. It was the old-fashioned kind that had to be pinned onto my dress, so it was kind of hanging off my boob. I felt like a dork for even thinking about that after what Ryan had just been saying.

I sighed and looked straight ahead. "So, I think I've done a smash-up job of making the conversation about as heavy as possible right at the beginning of the night, eh?"

Ryan chuckled. "I don't know, maybe we should talk about famine in Africa or something."

I did a face-palm and sighed. "Sorry. I didn't mean to . . ."

"Don't worry about it." He looked away from the road long enough to give me a small smile. "To tell you the truth, it's kind of nice to be able to talk to someone about it."

A single question had been burning in my brain since Ryan had come out to me two weeks ago, and I had officially reached the point where it could no longer be contained. "So, have you ever kissed a guy?"

Ryan made a startled, gagging sound. "Jeez, Heart, don't beat around the bush or anything."

"I'm sorry, but I've been dying to ask!" I balled up my hands into fists and pressed them both into his shoulder. "So, have you?"

"Have you?" he shot back.

"A guy? Yeah." Not in a while, but I didn't suppose that's what he was asking. "A girl? No. So, have you?"

"Kissed a girl? Yeah, in ninth grade."

Suddenly the Jeep made a sputtering sound and began to jerk while the engine roared up and down.

"What's going on?" I gripped the sides of my seat.

"I don't know." Ryan tried giving it a little more gas, but the Jeep was not amused. Abruptly, it went silent, and then all we could hear was the sound of traffic around us.

"Um . . . ," Ryan said.

"Does this happen a lot?" I asked.

He made a dismissive sound and tried to turn the engine over a few times. The Jeep probably would have laughed if it had actually been running.

"Now what?" Twisting around, I saw the angry face of the driver behind us. "You should probably put the hazards on."

Ryan poked the button, and thankfully, rhythmic clicking began. So at least the emergency systems were working. "We should get out of traffic," he said. "Can you come around and steer?"

"Sure." A bubble of laughter welled up in my throat, but I managed to turn it into a smile as I got out to run to the driver's side. To the left of the Jeep, cars were swinging wide to avoid the open door and revving their engines as they passed.

"Yes, we sense your distaste!" Ryan called to one car as it passed. "Thank you for your input!"

"Isn't it nice how everyone is pulling over to help us?" I asked as I got behind the wheel and shucked my silver strappy heels.

"I'm overwhelmed by the generous spirit of this town," Ryan agreed. He slipped off his tux jacket and the checkered vest underneath before pushing up his sleeves.

At first he tried to get the Jeep rolling alone, but it was obvious that wasn't going to work very well, so I called for him to stop and hopped out to lend my support, leaning on the open door frame and trying to keep the wheel straight with one hand. The whole thing should have been a disaster, but I kept wanting to laugh.

We finally got the Jeep rolling enough to get it to the side of the road. Unfortunately, that landed us in a crosswalk.

I burst into giggles at last, propping my now sweating forehead on my upraised arm. "At least if we leave it here, it'll get towed."

Ryan grinned. "Problem solved!"

We both laughed for a bit, leaning against the Jeep. A car honked at us, but still no one stopped.

"This is ridiculous!" I said. "Do they think this is performance art or something?"

"Do some dance moves," Ryan suggested. "Maybe someone will stop long enough to throw change."

And then, because sometimes the universe is kind but only when it can also be perverse, a van pulled toward the side of the road right behind us. The setting sun made a perfect glare off the windshield, so we couldn't see who was inside, but I could tell from the front that it was one of those big, cargo-style vans.

I clapped twice. "Oh great! Finally someone wants to help us, and it's a serial killer!"

"Well, it *is* prom night." Ryan was joking, but there was a faint note of nervousness in his tone.

The van finally rolled to a complete stop, and my heart squeezed in my chest. Thank you, made-for-TV-movies, for making me terrified of unmarked vans. I couldn't stand there waiting for my imminent death without at least trying to do something. Scrambling into the driver's seat again, I reached across for my purse. If the police were going to find my body later, I figured I should probably at least have 9-1 dialed into the phone.

"What the hell is going on over here?" a voice—a *familiar* voice—shouted from the van.

My pulse crescendoed and collapsed into my chest with relief. The voice belonged to Pat, which meant the Serial Killer Mobile was filled with the No Drama Prom-a Crew.

"Oh my God!" I jumped back to the street.

"Is that—?" was all Ryan managed to say before the doors opened and the whole No Drama group spilled out.

"What happened?" Cassidy demanded. "Heart, you look amazing! Hi, Ryan! What happened to your shoes? What is happening here? Why aren't you guys at prom?"

"Whoa!" Pat held up a hand. "How 'bout we stick to one question at a time, Cass?"

"The engine just . . . died." Ryan shrugged.

"Here?" Pat asked.

I pointed to the spot about fifteen feet away where we'd started shoving the Jeep out of traffic. "There."

Schroeder appeared at my left shoulder with his eyebrow raised. He looked . . . classically handsome in a tux, like an old movie star. I never would have guessed. "So you thought this was the perfect parking spot?"

"Yeah, it's pretty sweet, right?" I propped my hands on my hips and surveyed the area. "Should be easy to find later."

He ignored that, glancing down. "Don't your feet hurt?"

"Not as much as they would have trying to push a car in heels." I wiggled my bare toes.

He made a face but turned his attention to Ryan.

"Should we get her out of the intersection?"

I made an indignant sound. "Hel-lo? I am perfectly capable of getting myself out of the intersection!"

"Down, Lung. I was talking about the Jeep."

I rolled my eyes. What is with guys and calling cars "she"? I swear, if the state ever legalizes man-car marriage, there are going to be millions of confused women getting served with divorce papers.

But Schroeder, Ryan, and the rest of the guys were already braced around the Jeep, and I couldn't effectively scowl at any of them. The girls surrounded me, and the questions came fast and furious—mostly from Cassidy and her nuclear-powered vocal cords. I explained what I knew, which was approximately diddly-squat, and let them take over retrieving my stuff from the car.

In a matter of minutes, the Jeep was safely out of traffic and we were all climbing into the serial killer van. Turns out, it was a transport van for a day care. Tot University to be exact. It had seating for fifteen, three car seats across the last bench, and plenty of Cheerio dust in the crevices.

"Is this ride classy or what?" Ally asked.

"Whose van is this?" I asked.

"My mom is the director of this day care." Pat thumped the dashboard affectionately. "She is our official transportation sponsor for the No Drama Prom-a."

"Wow. This night just keeps getting classier and classier." I reached for one of the many seat belts, not completely sure I had the right one, considering there were approximately seven hundred ninety of them in the Tot University van.

"Classy with a *K*, maybe." Kim snorted.

A poke in the back made me turn around to see Schroeder. "You sure you're okay?" he asked, eyes crinkled with concern.

"Yeah, fine." I gave him a confused look. "My feet are a little worse for wear, I guess." Pulling one foot up, I inspected the black stains left by the blacktop and found a few grains of gravel to flick off. "Eww." I bet Audrey Hepburn never had to put up with this sort of thing.

"Guess you ended up No Drama after all." He smirked at me, and, in a dazzling display of maturity, I stuck my tongue out.

"I'm sorry, Heart." Ryan's voice brought my attention back to my own row of seating.

I dismissed him with a tossed hand. "It's fine. I just feel bad that we had to abandon your car."

He shrugged. "At least we weren't *actually* kidnapped by a serial killer."

"That's the sort of thing that could brighten up any day, isn't it?"

"We should get T-shirts made."

I laughed. "Man, how much would it suck to get kidnapped by a serial killer while you were wearing your 'At least I wasn't kidnapped by a serial killer' T-shirt?"

He burst into a loud, deep laugh. "So, as long as we don't end the night stuffed into a trunk somewhere, this is the best prom ever?"

"Absolutely."

Ryan patted me on the knee. "I knew you were the right girl to ask to the dance."

"Aww!" I leaned my head on his shoulder. "I really am the best, aren't I?"

Another poke in the shoulder had me turning back to Schroeder. "What's up, Pokey Pokerson?"

He drew back like I'd threatened him. "Sorry. I just thought you might want these." He held out a pack of baby wipes. "I found them in the back of the van."

I must have given him the are-you-crazy face, because he rolled his eyes. "For your feet?"

"Did your aunt give you a care package, too?" Ryan asked, and I giggled.

"What?" Schroeder looked utterly confused.

Blushing, I took the crinkly package of wipes from him. "My aunt gave me a little care package for tonight."

"It's full of lots of goodies." Ryan held up the cellophane bag, which I'd left in my lap after the girls handed me my stuff. The condoms were clearly visible against the side of the bag.

Schroeder sat back suddenly, looking out the window. He crossed his arms, and I could hear the *thump-thump-thump* of his heel on the van's floor.

I snatched the bag from Ryan. "Would you stop with the prophylactics?"

Ryan snickered. "You sound like a little old lady."

"Bite me." I pulled a baby wipe from the pack and swiped the end of his nose with it, before hauling a foot up to do my best to scrub off the street dirt. Because every girl wants to spend the first part of prom cleaning her feet. This evening was definitely klassy with a *K*.

10 In which I am aquatically assaulted and suffer a fashion disaster worse than the tiger-themed corsage from Troy

HEADS

The ballroom at the community center was a lot nicer than I'd expected it to be. Not that it would be hard to surpass a person's expectations of a community center. I'd envisioned dirty concrete floors and the smell of old gym socks. Instead, it had carpet and everything. The ballroom even had chandeliers—go figure. I guess it was worth the thirty-minute drive down to the smaller but much more affluent town to our south.

Despite the feelings of anxiety I'd had on the sidewalk, checking in for our table assignments went smoothly, although seeing my No Drama friends' names on the list gave me a little pang. Especially once I saw Ryan's name with their table number next to it. I'd given him my ticket when I'd turned him down.

At least the chaperones at the check-in table either hadn't noticed, or didn't care, that I was accompanied by a limo-ful of intoxicated seniors.

Tara did a decent job of including me in the conversation as we moved through the banquet room to find Table 20, our assigned spot. And Troy seemed a little more sober in the air-conditioning. Maybe I'd underestimated him. Maybe he was just plain hot in his formal wear. A sudden giggle bubbled up in my throat when I realized he was exactly the reason tuxes were called monkey suits. He did kind of resemble a gorilla in a suit.

I am a terrible person, and I am definitely going to hell.

I pressed my lips together and vowed to be more charitable.

So, when Troy asked if he could drink my ice water, I handed it over most willingly. A little dehydration was a fair price to pay not to be escorted by a fall-down drunk who was at least twice my size.

After the student council president delivered a blessedly short welcome speech, the salads were brought to the table. Our school administrators labored under the misapprehension that providing dinner in the same location as the dance would cut down on underage drinking. In fairness, there was almost zero drinking going on while the food was on the table—except in the bathrooms. But the number of people who showed up already sporting a blood alcohol level that would prevent them from legally driving was astonishing. I think that's what they call winning the battle but losing the war.

Dinner itself wasn't half bad, though, and Troy seemed too hungry to keep up his buzz at the ad-hoc bar in the bathroom. It was kind of pleasant, actually. I would have sooner died than say it out loud to my table companions, but I felt strangely grown-up being served by bow-tied waiters without my dad sitting next to me and some relative in a wedding dress at the head of the room.

Then, Olivia and Randi excused themselves to the bathroom, and once they were out of sight, Doug started scrounging in his pocket for something.

"Check this out," he snickered, clearly delighted with himself. I squinted as he slipped something small onto Olivia's dinner plate.

"What's——?" Austin leaned over for a closer look and guffawed. "Oh, that's fantastic."

Tara clicked her tongue. "What did you assholes do?" She stood up slightly to get a look of her own and squealed. "Eww! Is that real?"

"No!" Doug cackled.

"What is it?" I asked.

"A fake roach," Tara said, making Troy and Phil roar with laughter. "You guys are idiots!" she snapped. "Get it out of there."

"No way, you gotta leave it!" Austin said, putting a hand out to still her.

"Don't be stupid." Tara tried to reach again, but Phil caught her wrist.

"Come on, T, take it easy. It'll be funny."

Tara pursed her lips and narrowed her eyes at him.

I couldn't for the life of me decide who was wrong here. On the one hand, it was kind of funny, but on the other hand, Olivia never struck me as the kind of girl who would appreciate a good fake roach joke. I looked at Phil, but he was obviously enjoying the idea. Sometimes, my brother is a bit of a disappointment to the LaCoeur gene pool.

"Heart, tell 'em they're immature idiots," Tara commanded.

"Um . . ." Before I could declare myself, Doug was shushing all of us.

"They're coming!" he hissed.

Tara sat slowly, glaring at him, but she let the roach stay.

76

Olivia and Randi were too busy talking as they came back to their seats to notice what was lying in wait on Olivia's plate.

Despite my brother's insistent yanking on her elbow, Tara tried one last time. "Olivia, don't freak out—"

But the words were a total waste of breath. Olivia's blue eyes went wide with terror just as she picked up her fork and she screamed.

Not a squeak, or even a squeal.

It was one of those pure, gut-wrenching screams that horror movie directors probably dream of. A full-bodied scream that made her flail all her limbs simultaneously in what should have been a completely random fashion, but instead was somehow concentrated on the plate in front of her. She shoved it—and the whole table—with the kind of strength you hear about when a mother lifts a car off her child.

I, of course, was seated directly across from her. Through some complicated physics that I could never explain even with diagrams, the dinner plates all slid away from me as the table slammed directly into my abdomen. Air rushed out of my lungs, and I doubled over. Since my body was the handy blunt object that stopped the table's momentum, however, the water glasses, and the water-filled centerpiece on the table, all sloshed toward me, and a miniature tsunami of ice water poured across the table and into my lap, soaking the entire bodice of my dress and even sending a few ice cubes down my cleavage.

Through it all, Olivia's shrieks continued, completely drowning out Doug's efforts to explain that it was fake, even when he picked the stupid roach up and waggled it at her, shouting, "Fake! See?!"

I sucked in a breath, only to cough it out again as my crushed belly protested. Phil was the one who finally had the presence of mind to shove the table back again, sending Olivia skittering backward with a fresh scream, but I so didn't care about her at that moment. In fact, if I'd been able to breathe, I probably would have given the table a shove of my own, hopefully trapping Olivia under it, and then I would have put the rubber roach in her hair. Instead, I just gasped as my diaphragm did its thing, and pushed away from the table to swipe all the ice cubes off my lap.

"You okay?" Troy asked, patting me on the back.

I just groaned, because seriously, what did he think I was going to say?

"Oh crap," he said suddenly, looking behind me.

"What?"

"Your dress is all . . ."

"Wet?" I grunted.

"No. Like, ripped or something."

"What?" I went wide-eyed and tried to reach around back. Right away, I knew what had happened. The zipper on my beautiful vintage dress had separated. The slider was still secured at the top, but it was already unraveling below, starting at my waist. "Oh! Oh no!"

I stood up from the table, awkwardly grabbing my dress in the back with one hand to cover the gap, and made a beeline for the bathroom. Stars twinkled in front of my eyes as my lungs stridently protested that they were still running on backup power. I pushed through the dizziness, determined to get out of sight before I put on an unwilling topless show.

In the bathroom, I could finally slow enough to let my diaphragm catch up and managed my first full breath since taking the table in the gut. The stars winked out, and I sagged over to lean on the counter in relief. The move put more pressure on my ailing zipper, and I felt the fabric give a little more. I straightened and twisted to peer over my shoulder in the mirror, moaning when I saw the damage. It was the all-too-familiar zipper disease. Being a veteran vintage clothing shopper, I was well versed in the dangers of pre-owned clothes, and zipper disease was always a risk.

Over time, the teeth become worn down and don't weave together quite as tightly. A little too much pressure in the right spot, and *zoop*, you're baring yourself to the world.

"Damn it! Damn it! Damn it!" I muttered, and let my shoulders droop. Big mistake. It was only good posture that was keeping the rest of the zipper from falling slack. As I watched, the teeth separated all the way up to the slider, which I knew from experience was now very likely stuck at the top.

A toilet flushed, and Ally emerged, looking totally prom-worthy in her short black-and-white dress.

"Oh my God, Heart. What happened?"

In my obsession with the zipper, I'd almost managed to forget the soaked front of my dress. "You don't wanna know," I said miserably as chilly water dripped off my hemline to puddle on the floor. Somewhere in the vicinity of my navel, an ice chip was melting inside against my skin.

"How can I help?" Ally was already at the paper towel dispenser, yanking brown rectangle after brown rectangle of the stiff, barely absorbent towels for me. "Here." She held out a handful and set to work with a wad of her own, blotting at the dripping hem of my dress.

"I'm more worried about the back." I pointed over my shoulder. When Ally circled behind me, she gasped.

"Yeah," I agreed. "Can you see if you can get the zipper down and try again?"

Several minutes of struggle ensued before Ally left to recruit some more help. I waited in the bathroom, wondering vaguely if Olivia was still screaming. Stupid Doug. I hated that guy.

While I waited for Ally to bring backup, a few girls I didn't know very well came in and crowded into the handicapped stall together. I couldn't decide if they hadn't seen me or just didn't care that I was there, but they did nothing to keep their conversation quiet as they passed around whatever it was they were drinking.

"Did you see the way Olivia went off? God, that girl would do anything for attention."

"I know, she's so pathetic."

"I can't believe she even got nominated for prom court."

"It's just because she's going out with Austin."

"Seriously."

I wasn't exactly buddy-buddy with Olivia, but my ears got hot with embarrassment and anger listening to them dissect her.

"What about Tara Jansen's dress? Um, hello, you're not nominated for an Oscar!"

"No kidding."

"She thinks she's so great."

"Nala said she was in here before and she totally heard someone puking, and then Tara came out of a stall and rinsed her mouth out. Total bulimic."

"Ugh, that's so disgusting."

"She's not bulimic." The words were out of my mouth before I knew I was going to speak.

The girls crowded into the stall went silent. Then I heard some shuffling, and the lock clicked open. Two went for the door, but one looked straight at me with a sour expression. "We were having a *private* conversation."

I shook my head. "You really weren't."

"You should mind your own business."

"Seriously?" My wet, damaged dress had shortened my tolerance for stupidity. "I'm not the one gossiping in a handicapped stall about people I don't even know."

She glared at me, then turned to follow her friends out the door, nearly running into Ally and her backup as they finally returned.

"Whoa!" Ally jumped back.

"Excuse you," Little Miss Nasty Attitude snarled.

Ally looked at me as the door closed behind the cloud of snark. "What did I do?"

"Nothing." I rolled my eyes. "I think she put her thong

on backward." It wasn't worth my time or theirs to rehash what I'd overheard. I wasn't even going to tell Olivia or Tara. I had a feeling they'd both heard plenty of gossip about themselves over the last four years. You don't get to be a senior looking like custom-ordered perfection without earning a little jealousy along the way.

Besides, I had way bigger problems of my own to deal with. Like my naked back.

Ally had found a junior named Becca who worked on the costume crew. My heart and eyebrows lifted in mutual hope. If anyone would be able to fix me, it was Becca. Becca was capable of wardrobe miracles. Last year, when Len Greenwich told her she had to outfit the entire cast of *A Chorus Line* on two hundred and fifty dollars, she not only succeeded, she gave him change. Thirty-seven cents, as I recall.

Cassidy came in while the other girls were still doing battle with my dress. So far, the only thing we'd managed to accomplish was making Becca's and Ally's fingers sore and getting me smacked in the back of the head a few times when their fingers slipped off the stubborn zipper.

"Can we just pin it?" Cassidy asked.

"With what?" Becca asked. "I didn't think to bring any safety pins, did you?"

I thought longingly of my stupid care package from Aunt Colleen. The woman had given me matches, for heaven's sake, but not a single safety pin was in the little pouch of humiliation. I'd seen Becca do some creative stuff to repair damaged costumes midshow, but I didn't think bobby pins and lip gloss were going to be enough.

Ally left to hunt up some pins, and she was gone for so long, I was starting to think she'd forgotten about me. Becca eventually returned to her dinner with a promise to come back if pins showed up. Thankfully, Cassidy stuck it out.

"So, how's your date with Troy going?" she asked.

"Believe me, this is so not a date." I rolled my eyes.

"Not that you'd know a date if one came up and humped your leg." Cass hoisted herself onto the vanity counter and let her sparkly pink Chuck Taylors swing like a little girl.

"He was drunk when he showed up in the limo." I sighed. "Since then, I've been assaulted by a table, gotten a lap full of water and ice in my bra, and ripped my dress. Is that a date?"

She grinned. "Sounds like some of the dates I've been on."

I propped my elbows on the vanity next to Cassidy.

"Which is exactly why I don't date."

She just rolled her eyes.

Suddenly, there was a timid knock on the door. "Heart? Are you in there?"

Cass and I exchanged glances. It was a male voice. Definitely not Troy. "Yeah?" I called.

"Can you come out? We're going to fix you up."

After a moment of fussing, I emerged from the bathroom with Cassidy holding my dress closed from behind. It was one of the stage crew guys, Tim, who'd spoken. He wasn't alone. In fact, he was with Ryan. Guilt sent my stomach swooping toward my feet. Even though Ryan had been understanding about me accepting Troy's invitation, I'd felt awful about turning him down. And now, here he was, to see me in my exposed, damp glory. Fantastic.

"You found safety pins?" Cassidy asked.

"Nope. Better." Tim held up a roll of duct tape, extending the tail with a resounding *rrrrrriiiippp*.

"Duct tape?"

"It holds the universe together," Tim intoned.

"I don't want duct tape all over the back of my dress!" This was so not a Brigitte Bardot moment. This wasn't even a Lucille Ball moment. It was just plain sad.

"Don't worry, we have a plan," Ryan said. "Trust me."

"Let 'em try, Heart. You can't spend all night in the bathroom," Cassidy said.

They had to be joking. I glared at them all for a minute, but no one was laughing. With a sigh, I turned to show them the damage. "Fine."

In the end, I had a giant mat of duct tape, crosshatched and woven for maximum security. The shiny part of the tape was against my skin, with the whole expanse of the sticky side exposed to the inside of my dress. Of course, due to the sticky nature of the stuff, they couldn't get the two sides to line up exactly, leaving me with a thin strip of exposed stickiness mid-zipper, but it wasn't a half-bad job. The boys wanted to make it extra secure with a few long strips wrapped all the way around my torso, but I flat-out refused.

"Thanks, you guys!" I gave everyone involved a tight squeeze. "I don't know what I would have done without you."

"Flashed the entire junior and senior class?" Ryan suggested.

"Pretty much."

"Oops!" Cassidy said as she eased back from hugging me. "One of the baby's breath from my corsage got stuck to your tape." Her corsage was a single yellow rose surrounded by baby's breath. Ally's mom had promised to make all the corsages and boutonnieres for the No Drama Crew. Yellow roses for friendship. It was understated. Tasteful. And noticeably lacking any plastic tiger charms.

"Whatever. I don't even care." I waved my hands, making the stupid tiger charm on my own corsage bobble and dance.

"Oh. Well, then . . . here." She plucked off a few more and slapped them onto my back.

I laughed. "Thank you."

"All right. Are we going back to dinner, then?" Tim asked.

"Yes!" Cassidy and I said together. I couldn't even guess how long we'd sat in the ladies' room.

We walked down the hall to the ballroom together, laughing about what other improvements we could make to prom with the rest of Tim's duct tape, but when we reached the doors, they took off for the opposite side of the room where the No Drama Prom-a and all my other friends were sitting. With a pang, I turned instead for Table 20.

Maybe Schroeder and Lisa were right. I should have just gone with my friends like I'd planned.

11 Wherein I become performance art, and Ryan says terrible things that cannot possibly be true

TAILS

"The duct tape makes the outfit," Ryan assured me.

"I have a great idea!" Ally came at me brandishing a Kleenex. "We can stick this in the gap to cover up the tape!"

She looked so pleased with herself, I couldn't help laughing. "Yeah, that's gonna be so much better."

The zipper on my dress had given up the ghost as we climbed out of the day-care van. We hadn't even made it into the building yet, and so far I'd managed to turn my feet black pushing a broken-down car and practically exposed myself to the entire parking lot. Thank God it was only my back showing, and thank God the zipper's slide was still stuck at the top, or my strapless dress would have turned into a skirt in a heartbeat.

My friends could not stop laughing. It really was kind of funny, when I considered it, although I was considerably less amused than they were, since it was my back on display. The classiness was only increased by the duct tape repair job Ryan had managed to engineer with the help of his fellow techie, Tim, who had arrived just after us and parked a couple cars down the row. Tim was a guy who went nowhere without duct tape. Guys like that are the unsung heroes of the ordinary world.

"It might work." Cassidy brought me back to Ally's proposed decorative solution.

"Aren't I pathetic enough?" I asked.

"No," the girls said in unison.

I couldn't help it. I laughed. "You guys are nuts. I'm not putting wads of Kleenex on my back. I'll look like a vertical garbage can."

"Here." Schroeder interrupted us with his tux jacket held out for me to put on. "Let's at least get inside, shall we?" he said.

"Such a gentleman." Ally didn't sound pleased with that assessment.

"Such a fun ruiner," Cassidy corrected.

"Go 'head, Kidney, put it on." Schroeder jiggled the jacket at me.

It was a sweet gesture, but I smiled and shook my head. "That's okay. It's not like the entire prom isn't going to see my awesome duct tape repair job later, right?"

"Oh." He kept holding the jacket awkwardly, like I'd pulled the batteries out of him.

"Thanks, though." I smiled again before skipping ahead to put my arm through Ryan's.

"All set?" Ryan asked.

"Yes." I nodded. "And I'll do my best not to embarrass you any further as your prom date."

He laughed. "You're not embarrassing me."

"I'm going to be the world's most perfect nongay prom date in history," I whispered.

Ryan glanced around nervously. "Could you not say that so loud?"

"I didn't!"

"Okay, then maybe not at all?"

I made a show of zipping my lips and tossing the key. "Back in the closet with me."

"I think that's my line." He gave a sly smile.

"Whatever." I waved away his pesky semantics.

My brother and his entourage were ahead of us in line for check-in. He looked back at me and jerked his thumb at Troy, who was stoop-shouldered and sad-faced without a girl on his arm.

"Your fault," Phil mouthed. Then he grinned and slapped Troy on the back. "Don't worry about it, man. You can scam on the girls without dates."

"You're being gross again," Phil's girlfriend, Tara, said.

Behind me, Cassidy snorted. "Ignore him," she whispered to me.

I tried, but it wasn't easy until Phil disappeared into the ballroom.

At the check-in table, we got two little place cards with our names on them, surrounded by palm trees. We were assigned to Table 3, and a quick consultation with Cassidy told me they were at Table 4. Perfect. Things were finally looking up.

Prom's Moonlit Beach theme was visible, but not ghastly, with centerpieces of floating candles bobbing above a bed of tiny seashells in shallow bowls, and paper lanterns glowing along the borders of the room. Apart from a few paper palm trees I assumed were contractually obligated by a beach theme, the overall look was subtle, bordering on tasteful. Well, as tasteful as anything involving fake palm trees could be. We were sharing a table with a few other techies, including Tim, and their dates. I didn't recognize one of the girls, but the other two I knew well enough to say hello to.

Minutes after I sat down, I felt the first push against my spine. I turned to find Ally grinning at me. "You didn't say anything about seashells."

"What?" I twisted to see my own back, but of course I couldn't. Because I'm not a barn owl. And slapping around with my hand wasn't getting the job done either. I poked Ryan and made him report.

"You've got one of the little shells from the bowl stuck to your tape." He held up his thumb and forefinger about a centimeter apart to indicate the size of the shell.

"Great." I sighed.

Before I could finish processing that, I had three more stuck on, thanks to the quick work of Cassidy, Pat, and Neel. "You guys suck," I told Neel, who had the misfortune of being the last one.

"We're just making you look more fabulous," Ally called from the other table.

I rolled my eyes, but I knew I had to let it go. Two reasons. First of all, getting mad would only encourage them. Second, it was kind of funny. Okay, it was a lot funny. If the situation were reversed and it were any one of my friends with duct tape sticking out of her dress, I would be the first in line with handfuls of glitter. I got up from my table and slid into the empty seat between Neel and Schroeder.

"All right. Fine. But four seashells are not going to cut it. What else you guys got?"

Ally's eyes lit up, and instantly her hand went back into the bowl of floating candles to retrieve more of the tiny shells littering the bottom. Reaching around Neel, Kim plucked a petal from the yellow rose in her corsage and stuck it in the middle of my back. I stood up to give them all better access, and for the next few minutes all I heard was giggling interrupted by the occasional pressure in the area of my broken zipper.

"That's it!" Cassidy declared after a while. "No more room."

I reached back with a delicate hand to probe at what I could feel. I found more than a few seashells under my fingertips, along with what felt like bits of paper and flowers. I probably resembled the floor at a movie theater, but I couldn't help laughing.

"You look fantastic," Ally assured me.

"Thanks, you guys." After posing for pictures on a few phones, I told them I should probably go back to Ryan.

"Sorry about that," I said when I took my assigned seat. "What do you think?"

"It's, um, breathtaking." Ryan leaned closer, checking out all the additions to my dress. He laughed softly. "Oh man . . ."

"What?"

"Chase," he said, as if that explained everything. Like always, I had to do a mental double take to realize he was talking about Schroeder.

"What about him?" I did my not-a-barn-owl twisting thing again, once more failing to actually make my head rotate 180 degrees. Why was I even trying?

"He put his name on you. From his table card."

"He did?!" More pointless twisting on my part. "That idiot."

"Good thing he doesn't have a date. She'd probably be jealous."

"Please." I rolled my eyes. "He just thinks he's funny."

"Yeah, maybe." Ryan tipped his head.

"What's that supposed to mean?"

"Absolutely nothing."

He was obviously lying. I pointed my finger at him. "Bad prom date."

"All I'm saying is guys have strange ways of flirting sometimes." Ryan ran his fingertip around his water glass until it started to sing.

"Schroeder is not flirting with me." I shot a glance back at the other table and accidentally caught his eye. We both looked away.

"Maybe . . ."

"I think I'd know." I crossed my arms in defiance, even as butterflies began to emerge from secret cocoons in my stomach.

"If you say so."

Nervousness tiptoed down my spine. "Not that it matters. I don't date."

"Why is that, anyway?"

I sighed, very glad the other techies didn't seem to be paying us any attention. "I don't want to end up like my mother."

Ryan's mouth opened and closed like a fish a few times. I'd seen this before. No one quite knows how to phrase the questions they always have about my mother. He finally settled on, "Where is your mom?"

"Don't know." I shrugged. "She left right after I was born. Haven't seen her since."

"Why?" Ryan blinked. "I'm sorry, I shouldn't ask."

I laughed softly. "Please. The least I can do is a little quid pro quo for your . . . honesty." I glanced across the table, but still we were on no one's radar. "She was only nineteen when I was born. Eighteen for Phil. I guess it wasn't what she had in mind for her life."

"Jeez. Have you ever thought of looking for her?"

"Nope." I leaned back in my chair, feeling the faint lumps of my decorations through the thick mat of tape on my back. "Why would I want to find someone who doesn't want me?"

"Don't you wonder, though?" He squinted at me like a specimen on the microscope stand.

"Not really. I mean, sort of in an abstract way, but I don't remember her at all. There's nothing to miss. It's always been just me, Phil, and my dad. Well, and the infamous Aunt Colleen."

He grinned. "Ah yes. She of the condom treat bags."

"That's the one. Anyway, the point is, I don't want to make the same mistakes she did. It's easier to avoid the whole dating situation and not have to worry about it."

"What do you do if you like someone?" he asked.

"It's perfectly reasonable to have a crush on someone and not do anything about it." Ryan looked dubious, so I went on. "Crushes are free. I mean, who doesn't have a thing for Captain Jack Sparrow? Nobody, that's who."

"And here in the real world, where the rest of us live?" He cocked his head.

"It doesn't matter if it's the real world or fictional," I insisted. "Crushes are the best part of liking someone, and they are completely safe. You get all the benefits of fantasizing about someone, but none of the he-loves-me-he-loves-me-not drama. It's all the good parts with none of the parts that make you lie awake at night all angsty."

Ryan nodded slowly, and I thought I'd finally found someone who understood. Then he said, "You realize that's crazy, right?"

"I assume by crazy you mean genius."

He laughed. "What if someone likes you?"

The nervousness rekindled in my stomach, and heat crawled up my neck to my cheeks. "I guess they just don't." I managed not to glance back to Table 4, though I was convinced that Schroeder could feel the heat of my embarrassment even from the next table over.

"I think you might be a big liar, Heart LaCoeur."

"Bully for you."

Just then a piercing scream burst into the air from the far side of the ballroom.

"What the hell?" Ryan was on his feet before me, but it wasn't long before most of the prom goers were peering across the room. I couldn't see much over everyone's heads, but words filtered back through the room like an aftershock.

"Olivia Riggs . . . something in her food . . . drama queen . . . would she shut up? . . . out of here . . . never mind . . . oh, please . . . joke . . . forget it . . ."

And then I could make out Olivia Riggs, who was looking like the pageant queen she was in a teal, sequined ball gown, being escorted to the main doors of the ballroom by Randi Martinez. Both of them were chattering like angry chickens and casting death glares over their shoulders.

"Cheerleader drama," Pat announced from the neighboring table.

"She probably chipped her manicure." Ally wiggled her fingers.

Within minutes, everyone was back in their seats, and moving onto other topics.

I went on tiptoe to look for my brother, finally spotting him at the table Olivia and Randi had just stormed away from. He was laughing himself sick while Tara looked on with annoyance. She met my gaze for a moment and rolled her eyes. I wondered what it would have been like to be sitting beside Troy for whatever had just gone down. It seemed like I'd gotten off lucky being over here. Take that, Chuck E. Cheese's head.

12 Wherein Troy gets in touch with his primitive side, and I become a dance-floor casualty

---

HEADS

When I finally got back from my dress-repairing odyssey in the bathroom, Olivia had a smug look on her face. She was restored to full pageant dignity, except for the expression.

"You okay, Heart?" Troy asked. I couldn't help noticing he was looking a bit more cherry-cheeked again. Uh-oh.

"Fine." I smiled as I sat down. After all, it wasn't Troy's fault I'd been soaked and had my zipper break.

"Guess who just walked in," Olivia instructed.

"Uhh . . ." Doing a quick scan of the immediate vicinity offered me no clues. "Santa?"

Olivia's pretty mouth warped into a nasty smirk. "Amy."

I didn't know if she was trying to hurt my feelings or Troy's, but I was certain I didn't give a crap about my pity date's ex-girlfriend. "Okay," I said.

To my right, however, Troy wasn't nearly as unimpressed by the news. He slumped down in his seat and broke out in fresh sweat. The boy could use a visit to a doctor for that perspiration problem of his, I swear.

"Who's she here with?" he asked.

"I don't recognize him." Olivia inspected her nails as she said it, like she couldn't be bothered to check again. Someone should have hugged that girl more in her childhood.

"Where is she?" Troy stood up halfway and studied the entrance to the room. I looked, too. Solidarity? I didn't know. Troy found her before I did, though, and he collapsed back into his seat with defeat. "I don't know him either."

"It's probably her cousin or something lame like that," Phil said. I grimaced. Wasn't Phil the one responsible for Troy being on exactly the same kind of lame date with me? I sent a look of death at Phil, but he evaded my gaze. Why can I never kill my brother through latent psychokinesis when I need to?

"Should I go talk to her?" Troy started to get up again.

"No!" Everyone at the table was unified on that decision.

"No way, man," Doug said. "Don't be a pussy."

I winced again. The *P* word always made me feel like retching. I prefer to think that makes me dignified rather than immature, as my brother has suggested on a number of occasions. Brigitte never used the *P* word, I'm sure.

"I could handle it." Troy's eyes tracked Amy and her date as they made their way through the tables. "I could be cool."

"No. You definitely could not," Phil assured him, reaching over Tara to pat him on the shoulder.

"I'm going to the bathroom." Troy got up, and seemed to be aiming for the exit rather than the ex, but Tara elbowed my brother anyway.

"Go with him," she said.

"Only *girls* go to the bathroom in groups." Which was complete crap, since I'd personally seen Phil head off to the men's room with at least two other guys this very night. Granted, these were alcohol-based trips, but still. My brother was just being difficult. On purpose.

Tara didn't seem as annoyed as I would have been. "Fine. Then it's on your head if he goes after Amy when he comes back."

Phil mumbled something with a distinctly foul sound, but got up to follow his friend. I bit my lip and looked at Tara. "You think he'll be okay?"

"He'll be fine." Tara waved a hand. "Phil will give him a few shots to calm him down."

"Oh." Because what Troy needed was more alcohol. I reached to scratch at the edge of my tape pad. There was one little imperfect lump just below my right shoulder blade that was getting really annoying. And truth be told, I was starting to sweat myself with the thick application of duct tape covering my entire back.

A waiter appeared at my elbow to take my dinner plate, and I looked up hopefully. Dessert was always better than no dessert. And at least after dinner, I could hit the dance floor with my friends and stop worrying about Troy. I'd fulfilled my major obligations as a date, I figured. A few slow dances if he wanted to, and a picture in front of the sunset backdrop, and I'd be home free.

I'd nearly finished my piece of white cake by the time Troy and Phil returned. Troy had his jacket off now, which seemed to be cooling his head a bit, if his color was any indication. But the bathroom rendezvous had definitely not made him any more likely to pass a road-side sobriety test. He fell heavily into the seat beside me.

Phil clapped a hand on his shoulder, then bent low to talk to me.

"Keep an eye on him, okay? He's gonna be feeling no pain in a few more minutes, and we can't have him getting us all kicked out."

"Why would we all get kicked out?"

"We won't if you keep an eye on him."

"Phil!" I hissed, but he was already headed back to his seat beside Tara.

"Goo-oooood evening, everybody!" The DJ's smooth voice cut off any further attempts to snag my brother's attention. Though the fact that Phil was ignoring me was probably contributing to that problem as well. The DJ went into a spiel about the first dance, but he was talking so fast it was like listening to an auctioneer. Whatever he said seemed to do the trick, because as soon as he started blasting the latest dance hit, the floor was swamped.

"Come on." Troy stood unsteadily and patted me on the shoulder. "Let's show Amy I don't need her."

Which has got to be the most romantic invitation to dance a girl has ever gotten, right? Nevertheless, I took Troy's hand, only temporarily impeded from standing by the back of my dress sticking to the chair—thank you, duct tape.

I let him take me out on the dance floor, where he proceeded to do some moves I can only assume are part of a war dance in some lost tribe of the Amazon. There were a mysterious number of elbows involved, and a face that was probably meant to be sexy but looked more pained. Not that I wanted Troy to look sexy for me, but something less anguished would have been a nice change.

I scanned the dance floor, hoping to catch a friend's eye. This simply had to be seen. Preferably documented.

Finally, on the opposite side of the floor from where Troy was stomping, I spotted Schroeder. I nodded my head toward Troy and grinned. Schroeder smiled back before doing an impression of Troy's warrior dance style. I laughed and went into some awesome disco moves for Schroeder's benefit. He responded with some John Travolta, circa *Saturday Night Fever*. I cupped my hand against my mouth, miming a catcall, though there was no point in making any sound. It would be lost amid the throbbing bass.

A few of the other No Drama people showed up beside Schroeder and joined into the cross-floor dance-off once he pointed me out to them. I tried to keep my eye on Troy, but he was trained on Amy and her date like his eyes were an ex-girlfriend-seeking missile system. I was obviously just a prop in his pointless game.

Over on the other side of the dance floor, Ally started doing the Shopping Cart, so I did the Lawn Mower, which made her buckle with laughter. Then, just as I went down for another pull start on my imaginary lawn mower, Troy did one of his elbow-thrusting moves—right into the back of my head.

I wish I could say I was like a professional dancer, taking the blow and going on as if it was all part of the choreography, but that's not what happened. Nope. I went down on hands and knees so fast it was like I'd teleported. Right away, someone stepped on my left hand, someone else kicked me in the calf, and I got a mouthful of some guy's tux pants. Then, just as suddenly as I'd gone down, I was back up.

Troy had actually had the presence of mind to help me. I was shocked. I was also in pain, since he'd gripped me by my upper arms and hauled me up backward. For the second time tonight, I was seeing stars.

"You okay?" he asked in my ear.

"Yeah, fine," I grunted, rolling my shoulders. "Thanks."

"You've had some bad luck tonight. You should be more careful."

I stared at him, one hand pressed to the sore spot on my

head where he'd elbowed me, the other rubbing my opposite shoulder. Never mind the fact that I was still wet—down to my underwear—from my involuntary bath at dinner and my dress was being held together with duct tape. Yeah. Clearly, I was the one who needed to be more careful.

"Oh my God, Heart!" Lisa's voice announced her arrival the moment before she put her hand on my back. "I saw you go down. You okay, girl?"

"I'm fine." I smiled at Troy but let it drop when I looked at Lisa. For her I made an annoyed face and flicked my eyes at my oblivious date. "I'm going to kick Phil's ass," I whispered.

Lisa raised one eyebrow and leaned in to talk in my ear. "I *told* you to stick with the original plan."

"I know, I know."

Yet another hand landed on my back, and I turned to see Schroeder's concerned face. "What happened? Are you all right?" he asked.

"Fine," I said again, looking down. "Apparently, I'm very accident prone tonight."

"She got brained," Lisa told him.

"Let's get you some ice for your head." He took me by the elbow and started away from the dance floor, but I held fast.

"No, really. I'm fine."

His brown eyes searched my face. "You sure?"

I smiled. "I'm sure. Besides, I'm supposed to keep an eye on Troy." Glancing over my shoulder, I noticed that my date had managed to maneuver himself away from me and a few people closer to Amy. "Damn it."

"Why?" Schroeder asked.

"He's drunk." I rolled my eyes. "And Amy showed up with some strange guy."

"You should ditch him." Schroeder squeezed my elbow. "He's not your problem."

"Phil would kill me. And I don't wanna get kicked out."

He opened his mouth again, but shook his head and closed it without speaking.

The music changed to a slow song, and I turned to check on Troy again. He was staring in Amy's direction, of course, but suddenly he tore his eyes away, searching for someone—I assumed me. I looked back at Schroeder, who was still holding my elbow.

"I gotta—" I said at the same time he said, "Do you want to—"

I shook my head. "Sorry. I'll catch up with you later."

"Sure." He nodded, letting his hand drop away from my arm.

As I made my way toward Troy, Lisa pinched my arm. "You're an idiot," she said.

"Okay, I got it." I rolled my eyes at her. "Let it go."

"It's not that—" she said, but Troy cut her off.

"It's like she's not even looking at me." His eyes were shiny.

"Never mind," I told him. "Forget her. Let's just dance."

13 Wherein Ryan is a terrible date, and everyone comes to know the wonder of line dancing

TAILS

Convincing Ryan to dance was a little like coaxing a scared cat out from under a bed. I probably would have had better luck with a bit of turkey as a lure.

"How can you go to prom and expect to sit on the sidelines all night?" I demanded.

"It's called prom. That's short for promenade. That means to walk. I already walked in here. There is no inherent obligation to dance."

"There is so an obligation! It's implied."

"Well, I don't feel constrained by societal expectations."

"Ugh!" I groaned. "You are like the worst gay guy ever."

He went wide-eyed. "Would you stop with that!"

I looked around at the empty seats surrounding us. "No one heard me."

"I thought you were going to be cool about this."

"Well, I'm sorry, but I thought you were going to dance." I plucked my name card off the table and flicked it at him. "Besides, I'm helping you get more comfortable with your sexuality."

"A: I am perfectly comfortable with my sexuality. B: You were supposed to be cool about this, and C: Way to stereotype gay people." He held up a hand to tick off points on his fingers as he talked.

"Okay, okay. I'm sorry." I caught one of his hands between both of mine. "You're right. I'm being a bad date. But so are you!"

"What? How?" He spread his arms wide with palms upturned. Fakest innocence ever.

"You won't dance with me!" I whined. Audrey, Brigitte, forgive my lack of sophistication.

"I don't like to dance."

I leaned in close to make sure no one would hear. "How do you ever expect to meet a nice guy if you won't dance?"

He flushed, then gave me a superior look. "You realize this is like getting advice from a nun about how to meet men, don't you?"

"Just because I don't do it doesn't mean I don't know how."

Ryan snorted. "Yeah, okay."

"I *choose* not to date."

"It's almost charming how you're in such complete denial."

"Oh, shut up. We're dancing." I got up and grabbed both of his hands. And even though he was bigger than me, I got him to his feet, which was practically like him going willingly. I mean, he must have helped a little, right?

He groaned all the way, feet plodding like I was leading him to the dentist's chair rather than the dance floor, but he was just pretending, I could tell. He was going to thank me for dragging him out there. You're welcome, Ryan.

"Come on, live a little. It won't hurt," I cheered, giving him a perky grin and starting a simple step-touch rhythm. He didn't move, letting me do all the work with his limp wrists trapped in my grip. "Ry-yan!" I whined, bobbing my knees and letting my head droop back in surrender. "You are killing me. You're making the gods of dance cry."

He laughed, starting to sink his teeth into the role of stick-in-the-mud. "This *is* me dancing."

"Can you at least take that look off your face? You look like you're waiting for your execution."

Suddenly, he threw on a cheesy grin, tossed my hands off, and started hopping around, snapping and kicking in time. He looked completely ridiculous, but I whooped and hollered like he was Channing Tatum doing a striptease just for me. "Yeah, baby! Woo! Shake that ass!"

He collapsed into laughter, the cheesy grin relaxing into his natural smile.

"There you go! See? You're even having fun!" I tossed an arm around his neck and started a cancan kick line, which he completely refused to participate in.

Conveniently, Ally and Cassidy were nearby, and they were definitely not going to pass up a good kick line. Soon after that, the No Drama girls were arm-in-arm, kicking for all we were worth. Ryan eventually had to give in, doing some half-assed kicks but laughing about it.

The DJ was good, I'll give him that. When he noticed we'd started an organized dance, he faded in a new song with built-in choreography. I couldn't remember the transition step at first, but Lisa knew all the moves, and she was happy to take the lead. Ryan tried to escape, but I caught him by the arm and kept him next to me, fumbling through the moves. His booty shaking was hilarious.

I loved the feeling of finding more and more people had joined the dance each time we did the ninety-degree turn built into the dance. In one view, I could see Tara, Olivia, and the rest of the Dance Squad really shaking it to the beat. They even had little hand movements to go with the song. My brother was watching from the sidelines with a smile. In the next view, I laughed as the people who'd thought they were safe in the back were suddenly thrust into the lead. Another turn, I was treated to another dose of Ryan's awful hip rotations, but I had to admit, he seemed to be relaxing and enjoying himself at last. The last ninety degrees showed me most of my friends—the theater geeks, the No Drama Crew, the techies who'd shed their wallflower tendencies to get out and join the fun. Cassidy peeked over her left shoulder to catch my eye, giving me an extra butt wiggle when she saw I was watching.

We turned again, and Ryan leaned forward to shout into my ear over the music. "You got me dancing—are you happy?"

"Ecstatic." I grinned at him just as the song was ending.

"Now you have to do something for me."

"If it involves sitting down again, no."

"It involves me sitting down." I turned to protest, but he held up a finger. "Just me. That's what I need you to do for me. Go dance with someone else."

I shook my head, laughing. "I'm that lousy a prom date, huh?"

"Yes. Now go. Dance with someone who actually likes it." He grabbed me by the shoulders to spin me around and pushed me toward the nearest person, who was facing the other direction. I got a flash of blond hair and a black tuxedo jacket before I collided with him. It was Schroeder, who caught me in an awkward half turn.

"Sorry!" I gasped.

"You seem a little accident-prone tonight," he said.

A strange feeling of déjà vu swept through me, and I shook it off. "Guess so."

Schroeder looked over my head. "Where's your date?"

"He needed a break. Apparently, I wore him out." I winked.

"So you thought you'd body-slam me instead?"

We'd both started moving to the beat without realizing it, and now we were full-on dancing. Schroeder slipped a hand around my waist as another couple squeezed behind me. "Gotta keep you from knocking everyone else down," he said.

I stuck my tongue out at him.

"You're so pretty when you do that." He made a

screwed-up face at me in return, eyes crossed and upper lip sneered back.

"We should be prom king and queen, don't you think?" I sucked my cheeks in to make fish lips.

He copied my fish face, and we glub-glubbed at each other for a moment before breaking into laughter. We danced for a while, trying to restore our fish faces, but it was pretty much impossible to do fish lips and laugh at the same time, so it wasn't working. Then came the glorious moment when we both actually managed to fish it simultaneously. My eyes went wide with triumph, but I didn't dare move any other facial muscles for fear of losing my fishiness. Schroeder held up his left hand for a high five, and I slapped him a good one. He grabbed my hand when I made contact, and swept me around in a circle, all dancey-like. Pressed together like that, our fish lips were only inches apart, and it was too much. I caved first, laughing in a breathless way, but he only held out a few seconds longer, laughing too, and close enough that I felt his laughter as much as I heard it.

Ryan's speculations at dinner came back to me, and my heart got squirrelly—an activity I did not authorize. I found myself looking a little too long into his eyes. Brown. They were just an ordinary brown, but I liked them for that. Mine were brown, too. No extraordinary violet like Elizabeth Taylor, or sparkling green to make me feel more like a movie star. Just brown. It was a comfortable sort of color. Friendly.

Oh dear God, I was still staring at his eyes. I blinked heavily, but forgot to look away as I did it, so when I opened my eyes again, there they were. Comfortable, friendly, brown eyes that were making my stomach swishy.

"I—" I started, not knowing where I meant to go with my words.

"Let's turn our attention to the stage as your student council president takes the microphone once more." The DJ's patter gave me reason to blink again, and this time I remembered to lower my eyes. The music faded, then disappeared as everyone shifted their attention to the stage. Off to the side, the principal and vice principal were organizing rhinestone crowns, and I realized what was going on.

It was time to crown a prom queen and king.

Schroeder's hands dropped away from me, and he muttered, "I'll see you later," just before he walked off.

What did I do?

14 In which Troy leaves me for a life of royalty, and I learn the art of dance-based diplomacy

----

HEADS

I couldn't remember who was nominated for prom court, much less who I'd voted for. It was just not the sort of thing that concerned me. Maybe it should have, considering my brother was a big football-playing senior, but well . . . it didn't.

So, when the music cut off and the student council president came up to announce our prom court, I was just annoyed I'd have to stop dancing. Troy had disappeared into the bathroom again a while back, so I'd finally been free to dance with my friends, which was all I'd ever wanted out of prom.

"This ought to be good," Kim muttered, crossing her arms.

"Isn't Bethany nominated?" Cassidy reminded us.

"Oh yeah." Kim cupped her hands around her mouth and hollered, "BETH-A-NEEE!"

Bethany was one of those genuinely likable people who seem so rare. She had been in the fall play with us, though she claimed not to be able to sing a note, so she wasn't in the musical currently. Still, she was a senior, and one of the sweetest people I'd ever met in my life. Kind of shocking she'd even made it to the ballot, now that I thought about it.

Mild panic struck me as I contemplated a series of horrifying scenarios where Bethany was the butt of some cruel joke that was going to end in her getting doused in pig's blood or something. But it wasn't like Bethany was at the bottom of the social ladder, where she'd be likelier to be a target. And as far as I knew, she didn't have any ability to start fires with her mind. So, I was freaking out for no reason. Probably.

There were five girls and five guys to be named. Three princesses, the junior queen, and the senior queen for the girls, with all the matching royalty for the boys. The nominees were announced and asked to come to the stage. Every single person from my dinner table except me was called to the stage. I'd known I wasn't nominated, of course, and frankly, I didn't even want to be, but it was awfully hard not to feel like a loser being the only person out of eight who didn't have to make the long walk up to the stage. Especially when Troy was called. I mean, the guy was nominally my date, and here I was, in the crowd of common folk.

"I'm like the chambermaid to the prom queen," I murmured to Cassidy. She patted my back soothingly, but had to pull her hand away hard to get unstuck from my duct tape.

"Sorry," I said.

She shook her head and smiled encouragingly. "I think it's finally collecting enough fuzz and stuff to be less sticky. It was easier to get off this time."

I shook my head, eyes heavenward. "My life is a joke."

"Can we get this over with?" Kim said loud enough to get some nasty looks from people around us.

"Bitter much?" someone nearby sniped at her. I thought it might be the mean girls from the bathroom earlier.

Maybe we did need to consider a pig's blood/fire-starting scenario, if Snipey McSniperson was any indication. I didn't even like to think that such high school clichés were real, and yet, there they were live and in full color right in front of me. It was prom queen, for heaven's sake. I'm pretty sure no one was going to get into medical school on the basis of whether or not they were once the most popular person in their high school.

When the nominees for queen were announced, the second name was Amy Byers. Troy's ex. And even though Troy hadn't exactly been the prom date of my dreams this evening, I did feel bad for him having to stand on the stage and watch Amy step forward into the spotlight. Even from my position at the back of the dance floor, I could see Troy breaking out in fresh sweat.

"Poor guy." Cassidy laid a hand on her heart.

"I know. I feel for the big lug."

Onstage, Olivia took Amy's hand to complete the chain of would-be queens. Feelings of stabbiness washed through me, but then I remembered Olivia was used to clutching hands with mortal enemies while she waited for gaudy crowns. The girl had been doing pageants since she was six months old. I scanned the people on the platform. Of all of them, I really only cared about Tara and Bethany for queen.

Not surprisingly, however, it was a clean sweep for the cheerleading squad and the football team. Well, Olivia and Tara are technically on the Dance Team, but that's just semantics. Olivia was queen, and she accepted her crown with her big pageanty smile and a practiced wave to every-one. Austin, of course, was her king. Stop the presses, right?

"Ugh, I think I'm going to barf!" Kim faked heaving.

"I don't know," Neel said, tilting his head like a scientist studying a lab rat. "At least she's a professional. I mean, look at that wave." He raised his hand in imitation, tilting it just so. "If you're going to have a prom queen, it might as well be a pro, right?"

"Not bad," I said. "You might have a future in the Miss USA pageant circuit."

"Nah, I wouldn't want to crush Olivia's spirits with all my winnings."

"Very charitable of you."

He nodded. "I'm a real humanitarian."

"Goddamn Nobel Peace Prize in your future, dude." Pat slapped Neel's shoulder.

The DJ took over, soothing my eardrums with his smooth, professional voice, after the assault of microphone feedback and Principal Moss. "And now we'd like to ask that everyone clear the floor for the king and queen's first dance."

Everyone scooted backward as best they could, closing the already small spaces between us. I ended up wedged between a table and Kim's backside, with my head tilted to avoid the feathers sprouting from her hairpiece. Still, every time she craned her neck to see the dance floor, her feathers brushed against my neck. I squirmed until someone behind me touched my hip.

"Back up." It was Schroeder, beckoning me into a small space in front of him.

"Thank you." I stepped back with a full-body wiggle to shake off the ticklish sensation of Kim's headpiece.

"You looked like you were going nuts." His breath tickled the spot on my neck where the feathers had brushed, and I shivered. He hadn't moved back at all when I did, and every inch of me was aware of his proximity. If I had motion-sensor lights, I'd be lit up like the Eiffel Tower at night.

I shifted my feet, trying to find a comfortable way to stand away from Schroeder without seeming unnatural and still see the dance floor. The rest of the prom court would be out to join the king and queen any moment, and I'd never pass up an opportunity to watch my jock brother make an idiot of himself on the dance floor.

"So is Phil going to make you call him Prince Philip from now on?" Schroeder asked.

I grinned, looking back and up at him. "Oh, he already does."

"For some reason, I believe you."

"It doesn't seem totally outside the realm of possibility, does it?"

He laughed and stepped closer to me as yet another person made their way past us, putting both hands on my hips. "It's hot in here."

"Not if you've had an ice-water bath. I'm nice and cool." I patted my hand on the bodice of my dress. It was almost dry on the outermost layers, but there was still a definite dankness up against my skin. "Well, except for the parts where I'm covered in duct tape."

"You can't even tell," he said. "You still look really nice." Then he looked down and his hands left my hips. "For a girl named Kidney, anyway."

I elbowed him gently. "Shut up."

The song ended, and people clapped in a halfhearted way while the DJ wound into a well-rehearsed bit about bringing everyone out on the dance floor to join our prom court. It was another slow one. I don't know, maybe plastic crowns are supposed to make people feel romantic.

"Wanna dance?" Schroeder asked.

"Sure," I said.

With the floor already crowded, and the caterers working furiously to remove most of the remaining tables from the room, it was easiest for me to just turn around to face Schroeder. We took up a dance pose. That might be my favorite part about high school guys who do theater—they all dance the old-fashioned way, rather than the ham-handed way I'd suffered through in middle school.

"Hope you don't stick to my dress too bad," I said as he set his right hand against my back.

"I'll take my chances."

Schroeder was a good dancer. I already knew that from the play we did last year where we were partnered, but I didn't really remember how good until he pried his fingers off my dress to spin me under his arm. I smiled at him, remembering how much I'd looked forward to rehearsals back then.

"This is the way it was supposed to be," he said.

"What?"

"Prom. You were supposed to be my date, you know."

I blushed, glad of the heat in the room and the swirling lights on the dance floor to cover it up. "Oh really? What about your other six dates?"

He smiled. "We were ticket partners."

Prom tickets were cheaper in pairs (um, way to reinforce the stereotype that it's impossible to be fulfilled as a single girl in high school, school administrators), so the eight members of the No Drama Prom-a had all paired up to get tickets. I'd paid for mine, of course, but he was right, we had been partners. A fact I'd had nothing to do with, I'll have you know.

"Sorry about that. Are you all sad and lonely without me?"

"Nah, we took in Ryan." He cocked an eyebrow at me. "You know, your cast-off date?"

I scowled at him. "You make me sound like such a . . . I don't know, a player."

"I'm just teasing you. Take it easy." Using his right hand to guide me, he pushed me away for another under-arm turn.

When I came back around, I huffed at him. "So you just get to pick on me and spin away anytime I confront you on it?"

"Pretty much." He led me into another turn, this time adding a few more rotations to it before bringing me back.

"That's annoying."

He grinned. "I like to call it alternative conflict reso-lution. It's going to catch on for international diplomacy, mark my words."

And of course, I had to laugh. He was the master of the artful dodge. If he didn't want to give you a straight answer, you were never going to get one.

Schroeder managed to work us through the crowd to more open range in the middle of the floor, and we were able to do more than just a few underarm turns. He had me rolling out, then snapping back to a reverse hold. Finally, my vintage dress could do its thing, swirling around my legs and making me feel like Ginger Rogers.

I laughed as he whirled me through a twisting arm thing I could never repeat by myself. "God, I love dancing with you!"

His grip slipped, leaving my arm flailing, and he dropped the rhythm for a couple of steps. Shaking his head and blushing, he murmured, "Sorry."

I just shook my head, laughing even harder. "So much for Ginger Rogers and Fred Astaire."

"My fault." He settled us into a more sedate, standard rhythm. No more fancy footwork, and he seemed to be avoiding eye contact.

The song ended, and the DJ flipped into a pulsing backbeat that got a few screams of approval from various girls.

Schroeder rolled his eyes. "That's my cue to sit this one out."

"Oh." I startled as his hands dropped away from me,

feeling the shadow of his warmth on my waist. "Um, okay."

He turned, narrowly avoiding a collision with Cassidy, Lisa, and Ally as they stormed the floor, looking for me. I allowed myself to get swept into their stampede, joining in when they started to dance, but my eyes followed Schroeder off the floor. I couldn't shake the feeling that I'd done something wrong.

15 Wherein Ryan and I consider the nefarious motives of professional photographers, and Schroeder takes up the unwelcome new hobby of being a jerk

- -

TAILS

The line for the official prom picture was still long, but Ryan wanted to get it done. Personally, I thought he was just trying to get out of dancing more, but I wanted to get the picture, too, so I kept my thoughts to myself. The photographers were set up behind a series of black curtains that blocked the backdrop from view, so we couldn't see the couples having their picture taken. I suspected it was to prevent people from photobombing them, or harassing them behind the photographers' backs. But it also gave the illusion that you might be undergoing something more malevolent than a photograph.

"What do you think they're doing back there?" I asked Ryan.

"Taking pictures . . . ?" He said it like he wasn't sure of the answer.

"It's just so secretive-looking. Maybe they're making people sign a contract with Satan or something."

"Maybe they're fingerprinting people and demanding DNA samples," he suggested. "You know, under the pretense of identifying who is in the pictures for later."

I giggled. "Maybe they make you watch a sex education video before they'll take the picture."

"Then you'll just have to flash 'em your condoms and we'll skip the video."

While I laughed, Ryan stood on tiptoes, as if he could see over the top of the draped section. "Nope," he declared. "Just boring old photography."

"You having fun tonight?"

"Yeah." He smiled at me. "You know, apart from my car dying."

"And my zipper." I twisted to remind him of the collage everyone had built on my back.

"Don't take this the wrong way, but I'm a little more concerned about my car."

"I'm hurt." I did a fake pout.

"All right, who's ready for some picture-taking magic?" Neel's voice pulled our attention to the end of the line, where the entire No Drama Prom-a Crew was gathering.

"Hey, guys!" Ryan waved past the two couples between us and them.

"Hey!" Cassidy called. "Good timing! We were wondering where you were. Heart, we need you in the picture with all the girls."

Happiness cartwheeled in my chest. "Really?"

"Of course! Ooh, you should come back by us!" She beckoned us with rapid hand motions. Cass was normally a pretty animated person, but tonight she was on overdrive. I hoped there were enough exclamation points available in the area.

I glanced at Ryan. "You mind?"

"Nope." He took my hand and stepped out of line, waving the two couples after us ahead before joining the big group.

"Where are Lisa and Marcus?" I wondered. "I wanted to get a picture with the three of us."

Cassidy laughed. "I'd be surprised if Lisa gets him off the dance floor at all tonight." She did a decent imitation of Marcus's smooth dance style. The boy thought he was the love child of Justin Timberlake and Usher.

"Good point." I elbowed Ryan. "You could learn a thing or two from Marcus."

He laughed, a hard, barking laugh. "Yeah, right."

"He hates dancing," I told Cassidy.

She gasped, drawing back in mock horror with a hand on her chest. Whispering loudly behind her hand to Ally, she said, "If we don't move, maybe the alien won't notice us."

Ally laughed and joined in the whispering. "Do you think it knows we're talking about it?"

"Maybe we could drive it off with our awesome dance skills," Cassidy hissed.

"We might anger it." Ally shook her head and held up a staying hand to Cass.

"Are you enjoying yourselves?" Ryan asked.

"Immensely," Ally assured him.

"What are you jerks going on about?" Neel pushed his head between Ally and Cassidy.

The playful bickering went on for a while, making me laugh. I'd felt really good about my decision to come to prom with Ryan, but at the same time pretty guilty about ditching out on my friends. It was a huge relief that they didn't seem to resent my choice at all. Maybe I should have insisted on just adding a ninth chair to the No Drama table for Ryan. But he'd had tablemates all planned out with Tim and a couple other techies, so that wouldn't have worked. This was the best outcome I could have hoped for, I supposed.

Behind the girls, Dan, Pat, and Schroeder seemed to be

enthralled by something on Pat's phone.

"What are you guys doing?" I asked.

"Just checking the baseball score." Pat flashed his phone at me, displaying a dizzying set of statistics in some kind of grid.

"That's a baseball game?"

"They're called box scores, dummy," Dan said.

My sports knowledge pretty much ended with identifying the proper ball that any given sport was played with, though I'd been known to mix up a volleyball and a soccer ball depending on the design of the thing. "If you say so."

"What's the score?" Ryan nudged me closer to the guys so he could get a look.

I was about to accuse him of being the worst gay guy ever again but remembered to keep my mouth shut just in time. This secret-keeping business was not for me.

"Next!" The teacher assigned to chaperone the line called us forward, and Ryan took my hand again.

"Come on."

We slipped into the mysterious curtained-off area to find a giant blown-up photo of a beach at sunset with a hand-painted sign that read MOONLIT BEACH.

"On the marks, please." The photographer and her assistant bossed us around for a bit, getting us into the traditional pose with Ryan standing just slightly behind me, his hands on my waist and both of us turning our heads to face the camera. It felt forced and totally unnatural. When the photographer told us to smile, I burst into laughter.

"I'm sorry, I'm sorry! Hang on." I tried to compose myself, but the whole thing was just so stiff and uncomfortable. "Do we have to stand like this?"

I could see the photographer get annoyed, like watching a spill approach the edge of a counter. "It's a classic pose."

"Exactly." I shook Ryan's hands off and turned to face him. "I feel silly, don't you?"

"What do you want to do?" He looked suspicious.

"Um . . ." I tried a few different positions, but nothing felt right.

"We do have other students waiting," the photographer said.

"All right, all right." I grabbed Ryan's hand, forcing him into an over-the-top tango stance with our cheeks pressed together. "How about like this?"

"Whatever you say." She clicked the shutter, and the professional flashes burst all around us. "Exit to your right."

"No, wait! We're doing a group shot with the people behind us."

She sighed irritably. "Step to the right, please."

The No Drama Crew squeezed in, filling the curtained area well beyond capacity. The crabby photographer's face said exactly what she thought of this whole situation, and it wasn't positive.

"Why would you take a job at a prom if you hate people so much?" I whispered to Ryan.

"Beats me."

The No Drama Crew was determined to get their fair share of photography time. Neel took charge, arranging people into groups for pictures. The guys, the girls without me, the girls with me, each pair of ticket partners. Except when she got to Schroeder.

"I don't have one," he said.

"Oh, come on, Heart's right there." Ally pointed at me.

"She didn't come with me." He looked at Ryan.

"Oh my God, don't be such a pain in the ass," Cassidy said.

"She's not part of the No Drama Prom-a." Schroeder shrugged.

Embarrassment heated my cheeks.

"You're not going to get your picture taken by yourself, are you?" Neel said. "She's standing right there. Heart, get in there."

"I—I don't—" I could tell I wasn't welcome. There might as well have been a force field around him.

"See?" Schroeder shrugged again. His tone of voice was casual, but there was something about his posture that made it perfectly clear I'd abandoned him, and he wasn't happy about it.

"I don't mind," Ryan said. "It's not a big deal."

"It's fine." Schroeder stepped away from the X taped on the floor in front of the backdrop. "I don't need to remember being the only one without a date."

"I wasn't your date," I said automatically, and instantly regretted it. It had sounded more teasing in my head the nanosecond before it came out of my mouth. Out there in the open, it was harsh. Mean.

He didn't seem to react, though. Just crossed his arms.

"Are we done?" the photographer asked in an icy tone.

"Nope!" Ally declared. "Group shot! Everybody in! You too, Heart."

"I don't know if—"

"Oh, come on! You're exhausting me." Neel grabbed me by the arm and yanked me into the shot. I fell awkwardly against him as the camera flashed.

"Exit to your right. Next, please!" the photographer shouted.

I slid my arm through Ryan's, towing him out the exit and back to the lobby. "Come on," I said. "I want to go dance again."

He groaned. "Not again."

"Please?" I folded my lips into a tight line.

"What's wrong?" he asked.

"You were in there, right?" I nodded back at the photo station.

Ryan's eyebrows raised in understanding. "Chase?"

"Yeah." My face felt hot. Embarrassment, guilt, anger. Who knew exactly what emotional mix was cooking my head like that?

"I'm telling you"—Ryan looked over his shoulder as the rest of the crew emerged from the curtains—"he's flirting with you. I think he likes you."

I sucked in a breath and shivered before I could stop myself. Then I screwed up my face and grumbled, "Well, he's got a funny way of showing it. Now can we please go dance?"

"Do we have to?"

I looked back at my friends, feeling like there were football fields between us, instead of a few feet. "Right now? Yes."

"All right. But this is the last time."

"We'll see."

16 In which Troy obviously forgets who I am, and I plot my escape

--- --- --- --- --- --- --- --- --- --- --- --- --- --- --- --- ---

HEADS

Troy was now beyond drunk. He could barely make eye contact, but he'd reached a stage where he thought he was the coolest guy in the room. Phil was proud of himself.

"See? I told you he'd forget about Amy."

"You guys, he's like two seconds away from losing consciousness, or dancing on a table. Neither one is a good idea." I scowled at my brother and Tara, who were happily taking a break on some chairs near the dance floor. Tara's princess crown had gone lopsided, but somehow it looked intentional and devil-may-care on her. And this is why everyone is jealous of pretty girls and talks about them in the bathroom.

"That's why you're supposed to be keeping track of him."

"He's *your* friend," I reminded him.

"But if he gets kicked out, so will you," Phil said.

"That doesn't even make sense."

He shrugged. "Try it and find out."

"I hate you so much right now." I shoved off my own chair to go after Troy, who was standing directly in front of a speaker, laughing like a maniac.

I caught the big oaf by his wrist and tugged him gently toward the center of the dance floor. The chaperones were all on the perimeter, I reasoned, so it would be best if I kept him surrounded by a good buffer of other kids.

"Heart!" he bellowed, throwing his arms around me. I staggered against his weight. "There you are! Where did you go?"

"I'm right here," I said, still tugging on his wrist. I could make out a pair of teachers eyeballing him from the nearest corner. "Come on, buddy, you gotta come with me."

"Anything for you, Heart." He grinned and tripped over his own feet as we got a few people deep into the dancing. "Hearty Heart-Heart."

I wrinkled my nose. My name was bad enough without having it turned into some weird chant.

"The dance is almost over, huh?" I said brightly,

indicating my ugly tiger corsage like it was a watch.

"Then we can really go party!" he whooped.

My heart sank. I'd expected to chauffeur Troy home and pour him through his front door at the stroke of midnight.

"I don't know about that!" I was using my best fake enthusiasm, hoping to trick him into cooperating with my peppiness.

Suddenly he pulled me closer and wrapped his arms around my waist. The sheer weight of his arms was enough to trap me against his sweaty shirt. And just when my dress was finally starting to feel dry all the way through.

"I don't know how I could have gotten through tonight without you." His voice was thick.

I tried to ease back, but he didn't seem to notice, so I concentrated on keeping my feet beneath me.

"I mean it, Heart. You don't know what it was like having Amy rip my heart out like that. I couldn't imagine coming to prom with anyone but her. It's my senior year! Tonight is supposed to be the best night of my life, and she just threw it all away."

"Oh come on now, I'm sure there will be more important nights—"

He cut me off. "But then you said you'd come with me

and I knew. I just knew everything was going to be good again."

"Uh . . ." I tried to think of anything I'd done to deserve this other than show up in a dress and not punch him in the stomach for getting me a snarling tiger corsage.

"You've always been nice to me, Heart. Do you know that? Always."

That was when I started to panic. Just a little, but there was no denying it. He was giving me all kinds of bad signs. Signs that he was having . . . ideas. I squirmed back from him as far as I could manage and gave him my best friendly smile.

"Aww, thanks, Troy. Just glad to help out a *friend*." I really laid into that last word. If I could have managed it, I'd have punched him in the shoulder and called him buddy.

He wrestled me a little closer, hands clasped behind my lower back. I hadn't really appreciated how much material was in the skirt of my dress before, but I was extremely grateful for it now that Troy's fingers were in such close proximity to my butt. It was a built-in butt buffer. Maybe that's why the girls wore such floofy clothes back then. Men didn't know how to take no for an answer.

Around his shoulder (I definitely couldn't see over the

top of it) I could make out the basic shape of Amy and her date dancing not too far from us. Thankfully, Troy was facing the wrong direction, because Amy and her mystery man were up close and personal. Very up close and personal. So, when Troy tried to rotate us as part of his limited dance repertoire, I dug in my heels and tried to prevent it.

I was, not surprisingly, a total failure. I could tell the moment he laid eyes on her, because he sucked in a breath and swung me around so she was out of sight.

"Does she know I saw her?" he asked.

"I don't know." Peeping around his shoulder again, I saw Amy snuggle closer to her date and shoot a quick glance in our direction. "Yeah, I think so."

"How can she be doing this to me?"

"Don't worry about her." I shook my head. "Who cares what stupid Amy Byers thinks anyway? You're going to graduate soon and move on to way better things than her."

His big teddy bear's face was all crumpled up, but he actually seemed to be listening. "You really think so?"

"I know so." I patted him on the shoulder. "You're a great guy, Troy. You deserve better."

Looking him in the eyes seemed like the right thing to do, but instantly, I could see my mistake. He was so much taller than me, I had to tilt my head back to make eye contact, putting my whole face in a vulnerable position.

There was nowhere to turn when he laid a wet, alcohol-soaked kiss on me.

His tongue was like a fish flopping on a dock in my mouth, but hot instead of cold. I yanked back against his arms and tried to turn my head, but he just moved with me. Finally, I balled my fists and pushed hard against his chest. He stumbled back, looking confused.

"What's wrong?" he asked.

I wiped my mouth with the back of my wrist, trying not to shudder and let out the overwhelming *EWW!* that wanted to explode from my throat. So instead I just shook my head and held up my other hand in a silent *Stop*.

"I'm not . . . no," I said. "We're not like that, got it?" I gestured between us. "Friends, okay? No more."

"I thought—" he started.

"I know. But no." I shook my head again. "I'm sorry, but no."

"Heart . . ."

"I need a minute." I spun on my heel and wove through the crowd until I found Phil and Tara dancing under the disco ball.

"Phil! I can't do this anymore." Wiping my mouth

again, I shuddered. "Troy just kissed me. I want to go home."

"He did?" Phil broke into loud belly laughs. "That's awesome."

"It was *not* awesome!" I punched him in the arm. Hard. "In what world is that awesome?"

"In the world where it means he's getting over Amy."

"He did it right in front of Amy."

"Still." My brother shrugged. Tara at least had the good grace to wrinkle her nose.

"Still nothing. I'm done with this. I want to go home."

"You are completely overreacting. It was just a kiss."

"But I didn't want him to do it."

"Don't be such a baby."

"I'm not being a baby! I'm saying I want to go home."

"Stop freaking out. You're going to ruin prom."

"*I'm* going to ruin it? Are you kidding me?"

"Heart. It was a kiss. Deal."

I curled my fingers into tight fists, barely feeling the bite of my own nails into my palms. "Don't you even care what I want? I'm your sister."

"Yeah, and Troy's my friend. He wouldn't hurt anyone. He probably thought you wanted it."

"Phil!" Tara put up a token protest, but I didn't miss

the fact she was still dancing with him.

My chin started quivering, and I knew I had to get away before the angry tears breached my lids. I turned and rushed toward the bathrooms, desperate to get out of anyone's sight before I let myself cry.

But then, just outside the ballroom doors, I came across Cassidy and Ally sitting in a couple of wingback chairs near the photo backdrop where the professional pictures had been going on all night.

Ally had her shoes off and one foot propped up to rub at a sore spot on her ankle, but she let her foot drop back to the floor as soon as she saw me. "What's wrong?"

And that's when I burst into tears.

"Oh my God. What happened?" Cassidy got to her feet, putting an arm around my shoulders.

After a few shuddering breaths and some serious blotting of my eyes, I managed to tell them what happened.

"I'm sorry, Heart, but your brother can be such a dick sometimes," Cassidy said when I was done.

My instincts rushed to defend him. "He's just giving me crap. He always does."

Ally shook her head. "I don't think this qualifies as giving you crap."

I shook my head. "Whatever. That's just how he is."

"You mean . . . a dick?" Cassidy supplied.

"No." I felt fresh tears ready to join the fray, so I rolled my eyes up toward the ceiling, refusing to blink. "Never mind. I'm just . . . it's been kind of a rough night."

"That so sucks." Ally made a sad panda face. "If it makes you feel any better, my feet are absolutely killing me."

I laughed. One of those thick, tear-clotted laughs, and finally let myself blink. A tear escaped down my left cheek, and I wiped it away tiredly. "Not really."

"Seriously. Look." She extended one of her feet into the air, showing off three blisters in a row around the back of her heel, and another one near her pinkie toe.

I stared at her. "I just had the most disgusting kiss in the history of kisses."

Cassidy laughed and rubbed my back. "I'm sure it was bad, but come on, Heart."

"I'm serious! Troy just shoved his tongue in my mouth. It was like being Frenched by a German shepherd."

"Troy kissed you?" Schroeder's voice came from behind me.

Of course. Why not?

I turned, shaking my head. "More like mauled me."

"Are you okay?" He reached toward me but couldn't

145

seem to pick a landing spot for his hands.

"I'm fine." I sniffed and wiped my eyes. "It was just gross. I'm going to go . . . rinse my mouth out with soap or something." Heading for the bathrooms with determination, I didn't notice Schroeder trotting up to catch me until he was close enough to touch my arm.

"Hey," he said. "You sure you're okay?"

I tried to nod, but my eyes were burning again. I was going to cry, I knew it. I looked down, pressing my fingertips under my eyes.

"Whoa, um—okay." He put one hand on my shoulder. "Did he, like, hurt you?"

"No," I squeaked, swiping angrily at my eyes. "I'm fine."

"You don't look fine."

"Shit," I whispered, clenching my fists. I tried to take in a breath that would end all my tears, but of course, no such thing exists.

"Come here." Schroeder guided me closer until he could wrap me into a hug with my face pressed against his chest. I left my arms hanging limp at first, afraid to give in to the self-pity and anger, but when he pressed his fingertips into the tight muscles at the back of my neck just right, I relaxed into him, looping my arms around his waist.

"Do you want to tell me what happened?" he asked after I'd managed to get my sniffling to a minimum.

So, I told him about Troy, and about Phil's unhelpful reaction after. His fingers dug in just a little harder when I talked about Phil.

"That's not cool," he said. "Why was he being such a—"

"Jerk?" I supplied.

"I guess that'll suffice."

"I don't know." I turned my head, letting my cheek rest on him. "He's been drinking all night."

"Hmm."

I didn't know what that meant, but I didn't really want to talk about it, anyway, so I just let it go. Closing my eyes was much easier. Just existing was good enough for the moment. I hadn't been able to do that since I'd started pinning up my curls hours and hours ago.

"Are you worried Troy's gonna try . . . ?" He left it hanging, but I knew what he was asking.

"God, I hope not." I sighed and sagged into him a little harder. "With any luck he'll pass out soon."

Schroeder laughed softly, the sound of it vibrating through me from his chest. "You're really having a crappy night, aren't you?"

"I've had better." I sighed again. "Maybe I should just

call my dad to come and get me."

"Why don't you just come with us after the dance?" he asked. "I don't know if you heard, but we've got a pretty sweet ride tonight."

I tilted my head back to look at him, confused. I had no idea how they'd all gotten here.

"It's a fifteen-passenger day-care van." He nodded, smug. "Oh yeah."

For some reason, I wasn't surprised. Like I'd known what he was going to say already, but his expression made me laugh. "Aww, I'd feel so at home in that. My dad drives a big panel van, too."

"See? It's fate."

"I don't believe in fate." It was automatic. My response since I'd decided not to let my maternal genetics and my porn-star name choose my future for me.

"Why not?"

"I don't like the idea that I can't control the outcome of something. Your choices should be the only influence in your own life."

"Doesn't leave much room for being surprised. Or magic."

I eased back from his embrace, smiling up at him. "You believe in magic?"

He looked at me like I was nuts. "You don't?"

Laughing, I shook my head at him. "You're a strange one, Schroeder."

"Well, whatever." He shrugged. "Just come with us."

"That actually sounds perfect." I pressed my palms into his cheeks for a second. "I'll tell Phil he can be Troy's boyfriend for the rest of the night."

"Good." He grinned. "Feel better?"

"Not quite." We weren't too far from the bathrooms, so I pulled away from him so I could get a drink from the fountain. Even though he was watching, I swished and spit three times before I was satisfied. It was very ladylike, though. Audrey would have approved.

"Better?" he asked when I straightened up.

"A little." With no other option, I dabbed at my mouth with my fingertips.

"That bad, huh?" Schroeder smiled a little but seemed distracted by something on the floor, so I couldn't read his expression.

"Imagine someone stuffing a kitchen sponge soaked in dishwater and vodka in your mouth. Only first they put it in the microwave for a minute and a half."

He recoiled. "That's, um, descriptive."

"If that's what he's been doing to Amy for the last six

months, I'm not surprised she dumped him." I shuddered.

"Harsh. You're a tough critic."

"Well . . . it was bad."

He looked at me squinty-eyed for a second, and hesitated twice before speaking. "Do you know what it takes for a guy to actually try to kiss a girl?"

I rolled my eyes. "Believe me, that was totally effortless on his part. No thought involved."

"You don't know that."

"I was there."

"I'm just saying, it's not that easy. You're really putting yourself out there as the guy."

"Do you go around kissing a lot of girls you're not sure want to be kissed?" I raised an eyebrow. "I think that's called first-degree sexual assault."

"Believe me, it's hard to tell with some girls."

"Well, I'm completely positive I was giving Troy the 'Don't kiss me' vibe, so this one's on him." I wiped my mouth with the back of my wrist for good measure.

"You do have that vibe down pretty well." Schroeder sighed and looked down the hall.

He seemed annoyed, or sad maybe. So I nudged him with my elbow. "Come on. Let's go back to the dance."

"You sure?"

"Yeah. I'm just going to avoid Troy for the rest of the night. No problem."

"You'll be like a prom ninja." He smiled slightly.

Relief made me grin. "And then you can whisk me off in your mighty day-care van and rescue me from the evil troll."

He did a slight bow. "Consider it done."

17 Wherein I have *all* the feelings, and it's entirely Ryan's fault

----

TAILS

Ryan was true to his word—he didn't dance again. But luckily, my girls were more than willing to take his place. The DJ had switched to an almost pure dance beat, spinning all the latest music into an endless stream of sound that pushed my endurance to the limit.

It was so much fun.

I'd abandoned my shoes ages back, and my feet were probably just as black as they had been when I'd helped Ryan move his Jeep, but it didn't matter. Most of the girls were barefoot by this time. Ryan and some of the other crew members were more than happy to stand guard over our growing pile of high heels and purses. We'd shoved them all under a table where the wallflowers could sit on chairs and pretend they had a vital function that forbade them from dancing.

Occasionally, I shimmied over to Ryan and held on to his hands to dance while he sat. He was good about it, doing a hideous overbite and lots of chair swaying, but he never stood.

I'd been weaving in and out of groups for a while, dancing with anyone who was willing, even Phil and Tara. Troy, my forsaken pity date, was moping on the sidelines, but when I offered to dance with him, he just shook his head.

"Nah, that's all right," he said. "My feet are killing me in these shoes."

"Mine, too." I held my bare foot aloft and wiggled my toes.

He smiled. "That's funny."

"You doing okay tonight?" I rested my hand on his shoulder, feeling a twinge of guilt for leaving him alone on prom night.

"Yeah, it's not so bad." He looked up at me, red cheeked and sweaty in the hot ballroom. "You know my girlfr— Amy showed up with somebody else."

I wrinkled my nose. "I heard." Tara had told me earlier in the bathroom when I ran into her. "Sorry."

"I don't even know who the guy is."

"I'm sure he's a complete jerk."

Troy laughed. "I bet you're right." Then the laughter dissolved from his expression. "There she is." He looked past me.

"Where?" I whirled, searching the dance floor for Amy Byers. It wasn't hard to spot her. She was dancing with some tall, dark-haired guy close enough that Troy wouldn't miss her. I looked back at Troy. "Dude, you could totally take that guy."

"You think I should?"

"No!" I spun back to shake my head at him. "I'm just saying."

He squinted at the dancing couple. "You're right. I could pound that guy into the floor."

"You're not going to, though, right?" I gave him a stern look.

"Naw . . ." It wasn't convincing.

I did my best teacher voice. "Troy . . ."

He smiled. "Yeah, all right."

Dodged that bullet. What was I thinking telling a big lug like Troy he could take down the enemy? "Tell you what," I promised him. "If I can figure out a way, I'll kick him in the shins for you."

He smiled softly. "You're a nice girl, Heart."

"And here I was trying to be mean."

"Thanks."

"No problem." I bent over to give him a quick hug and caught a whiff of the alcohol on his breath. Thank God he was riding in a limo tonight. I straightened up and held up my fists in a boxing position. "I'll get him if I can. Promise."

The song changed to one of my favorites and I sprang to my toes, peering through the crowd for my friends. Kim's feathered updo was hard to miss. I shouted a good-bye to Troy and wiggled my way to join the girls in some serious dancing.

Overhead, the DJ's light displays were spinning, sending pockets of color flying around the ballroom while a small disco ball rotated at the front of the room, barely penetrating the crowd in comparison to all the colored lights. I whirled with the lights, letting the people blur in my eyes into blobs of bright colors. I spun long enough to make myself dizzy, and I had to grab Ally's arm for support when I stopped.

She laughed at me, grinning. "Smooth!" she shouted over the music.

When my vision slid back into focus, I noticed

something over her shoulder that made my heart drop into my stomach. It was Schroeder and a senior girl from the orchestra. Her name was Kathryn and she was beautiful, in a serious, scholarship-winning way. Smooth, dark-blond hair and the kind of profile you see in classic paintings.

They were dancing, closer than we'd been earlier. Not in the traditional dance pose, but like they were in a club. He had his hands on her hips, and she had her arms extended over his shoulders. They moved well together, I realized as my chest went tight. She was slinky and lithe like a ballerina gone bad, and he could move his hips in a way that would make most high school guys too self-conscious.

"What's wrong?" Ally peered at me, and I realized I was holding a death grip on her shoulder. "You gonna puke or something?"

I tore my eyes away from Schroeder and Kathryn, and looked into Ally's concerned face. "Sorry." I let go of her shoulder. "I'm fine."

"Do you need to sit down?"

With evil minds of their own, my eyes went back to Schroeder just in time to see him bend down to speak in Kathryn's ear. She tossed her head back, laughing. A lump closed my throat.

"I'm gonna go." I flapped my hand to a vague destination, talking to Ally but unable to look away from Kathryn's shifting hips. "I'm gonna . . ."

"Go." Ally gave me a gentle push. "You need to cool off."

I nodded and started toward the table where I'd left my shoes, finally tearing my eyes away from Schroeder and Kathryn when I almost knocked over another couple.

"I've got a bone to pick with you, mister," I called out to Ryan long before I reached the table where he was currently standing guard alone.

"If this is about more dancing, you can stop. I'll come back, I promise." Ryan held up both hands in supplication.

"No. This is about"—I screwed up my face and stamped one foot in frustration as I searched for the right words—"you made me . . . think about things."

"What?"

I dropped into the chair beside him and crossed my arms. "I was perfectly fine, and then you said that crap about Schroeder, and now I'm . . . I . . . ugh."

Ryan pressed the tips of his forefingers together, twisting them and making kissy sounds.

"Oh my God, are you ten?" I elbowed him.

He laughed. "You're having . . . thoughts?"

"*And* feelings. Damn it, Ryan. Feelings! This is not on my agenda."

"You said you don't like people."

"Well, I don't like *you* very much right now."

He grinned, utterly remorseless. What is it about people that makes them so enjoy other people's suffering?

"So, what happened?" he asked.

I sighed. "Well, first, when we were dancing, there was . . . I don't know . . . a thing."

"A *kissing* thing?" He did his finger twisty thing again, drawing out the word kissing like a string of saltwater taffy.

"No! Just an . . . eye thing."

"No! Not an eye thing!" He gasped, covering his heart with one hand. "I hope you used protection."

I snorted an involuntary laugh. "Shut up. It was there, okay?"

"And?"

"And then he was all weird during pictures, and now I have to think about that, and, like, wonder if it has something to do with me."

"And?"

"And you obviously suck donkey balls for making me have all the feelings. You're probably the worst prom date ever, but I'll have to check with Guinness on that and get back to you."

"I didn't make you do anything. You already had 'the feelings'"—he did air quotes—"before I got here."

"That is *not* true." I poked him in the lapel. "I was perfectly fine being friends with Schroeder—"

"Which is obviously why you have a cute little nickname for him," he interrupted.

"He looks like Schroeder. Hello?" Twiddling my fingers across an imaginary piano, I gaped at him. "What's weirder is that no one else noticed before."

"Whatever helps you sleep at night." He rolled his eyes. "So, you're all bent out of shape over some eye contact, is that about right?"

"No." I dropped into the chair beside him, hard enough to knock my teeth together. "I just saw him dancing out there with Kathryn Taylor."

He didn't have anything to say to that, but he leaned sideways in his chair, trying to get a glimpse.

"And even if he *did* like me, he obviously doesn't anymore, but *you* made me think about it, and I didn't even know before, and—God! I'm just . . . ugh!" I dropped my head in my hands.

Ryan patted my back. "There, there, little Pinocchio.

Now that you're a real girl, you were bound to have emotions."

I let one hand drop so I could glare at him. "I hate you."

He grinned. "You love me."

"Why did you have to tell me, anyway? I was perfectly happy."

"Sure you were."

"I was!" I sat up to look him in the eye. "Why does everyone think you have to have a boyfriend to be happy?"

"I don't think that." He held out upturned palms. "I mean, I better not, right? Look at me."

I twisted my mouth in thought. "Okay, but you *just* said I wasn't happy, so . . ."

"True."

"I was happy."

"Forbidding yourself from being interested in anything resembling a relationship is not the same as not needing a boyfriend."

"Ugh, maybe you are gay after all." I crossed my arms.

"What's that supposed to mean?"

"Well, you're into sports and you hate dancing, but now here you are giving me relationship advice."

"You have way too many stereotypes in your head."

"All right. I'm sorry. You're right." I sighed. "I'm not being the best nongay prom date in the world right now, am I?"

"Nope." He shook his head.

"Okay, okay. I'll do better."

"I have a great idea how you can start."

"Lay it on me."

"Go apologize to Chase for ditching out as his date."

"How is that supposed to help?"

"It'll make him feel better, which will make you feel better, which will make you a better date."

I raised my eyebrow at him. "Why can't I just tell him off instead? That would make me feel a lot better."

"I have my reasons." Ryan steepled his fingers beneath his chin.

I sighed. "Fine, but I'm pretty sure he doesn't want to hear from me right now." I was afraid to check the dance floor. "And he's probably sucking face with Kathryn, anyway."

"I doubt it." He leaned over again, scanning the dance floor. "Nope. No face sucking in sight."

"It's not like I can just go over and cut in on their dance."

"They're done."

I looked up and saw Schroeder making his way toward the doors.

"Go." Ryan shooed me off.

As much as I didn't want to do it, I ran after him. The dance wasn't over yet, but the floor was already less full than it had been, so it didn't take long to catch up.

"Schroeder!" I meant to only touch his back, but I underestimated my speed and ended up shoving him.

"What the hell?" He stumbled forward two steps before he could right himself and look back at his attacker—me.

My hands flew to my mouth. "I'm sorry! I was just trying to—" I shook my head. "I swear that was a complete accident."

He made an annoyed face. "What'd you want?"

I reached out with both hands palms up as if waiting for him to grasp them. "I want to apologize."

"You already did."

"No, not for hitting you." I scrunched up my face, wishing I hadn't chosen the word "hitting." "I owe you an apology for ditching you."

His face went still, carefully neutral. "Oh?"

"Yeah, it wasn't cool of me to bail on the No Drama Prom-a Crew. And especially you, since we had the tickets together and everything."

"No big deal." He looked away and shrugged. It was a big fat liar's shrug.

All I wanted to do was argue. I wanted to snap back about how he sure was acting like it was a pretty big deal, and if that wasn't what was making him act like a jerk, then maybe he was the one who owed *me* an apology. But I thought of Ryan, and I decided to make nice. Think Zen, Heart. *Om.*

"I should have come with you," I said. "All of you."

His eyes flitted back to mine, but he didn't say anything.

"I mean, it's been fun with Ryan, but it's not the same." I stepped closer and leaned in as if to tell him a secret. "He's a terrible dancer."

That earned me a smile, at last. "Yeah, I noticed that."

"Anyway, I just wanted to say I'm sorry, and I hope you're not mad."

"Why would I be mad?" he asked.

I pressed my lips together to keep from launching into a litany of all the ways he'd shown exactly how mad he was, and instead took a breath. "So . . . we're cool?"

"We're cool."

An awkward silence fell between us then, and we both looked everywhere but at each other. It seemed like the sort of occasion that should end in hugging it out, but I couldn't picture doing that.

"I saw you dancing with Kathryn," I said.

"Yeah?" The word lifted, hopeful.

"She—she's a good dancer."

"She is. You don't think of the orchestra people as having any rhythm."

A snort jumped out of me before I could hold it back, and I clapped my hand over my mouth in embarrassment, crushing my drooping, pinned-on corsage in the process. It was a running joke among the actors in the musical that the pit orchestra members were slightly lacking in rhythm. Or, you know, completely unable to keep time. Every year, the school had to hire a professional drummer for the three days of the show because no one could keep time well enough to trust the entire production to the student orchestra. With my hand pressed over my lips, I could hide my smile, though there was nothing to be done about my eyes, which I could feel were wide with stifled laughter.

When I could control myself enough to speak, I managed to get out, "That's not nice."

Schroeder grinned. "Kathryn didn't think so either."

"You did not say that to her!" I swatted him in the shoulder.

"I'm kidding! Relax."

This was the Schroeder I knew, and I was surprised at how relieved I was to see him. Maybe I'd been overreacting before and he really wasn't pissed off at me. Maybe the photographer had rubbed him the wrong way and he just wanted to get out of there. I ran over the incident in my mind. Yeah, okay, there was definitely more to it than that, but at least he seemed ready to get back to normal now.

"So, next year, if we're going to have a repeat of the No Drama Prom-a, and we happen to be ticket buddies again, and you happen to get asked to the dance by two other guys . . . ," he prompted.

I bit my lip. "I'll tell them to go with each other and count me out."

He smiled. "You wanna go dance again before they shut this place down?"

"Yeah." I nodded. "I'd like that."

18 In which my brother practices his sales pitch, and I am suckered

HEADS

The DJ gave us a two-song warning for last dance, and I pumped my fist in the air. I'd successfully avoided Troy since abandoning his gasping fish tongue on the dance floor, and now the end was in sight.

I'd stuck to my friends like glue, trying to keep someone taller than me between myself and the rest of the dance floor as much as possible. Schroeder was being particularly obliging in this ruse of mine, always checking over his shoulder for me and blocking me from view whenever he could. I could have kissed him. Overall, it had been an extremely successful strategy, and I was finally in the home stretch.

And that's when Phil snuck up on me from behind and

slithered his hand around my shoulders. "So, we're obviously going to Blanchard's for the after-party."

I tried to shrug his arm off. "*You* might be, but I'm not."

"Why not?"

"Um, besides the fact that Troy tried to stick his tongue down my throat earlier? Gee, let me think . . ." I tapped my finger against my chin.

"You're still being a psycho about that?"

"Yeah." I crossed my arms. "I'm not going." Across from me, Schroeder and Cassidy looked concerned, but I shook my head at them. I knew they couldn't hear what we were talking about over the music, but I was certain I had this in hand.

"*Everybody's* going," Phil said near my ear.

"If everybody jumped off a cliff, would you?"

"If there were a kick-ass party at the bottom of the cliff, I absolutely would."

"God, you suck."

"I told you, you don't have to call me God. My Lord will be just fine."

I punched him in the arm. Not hard enough to do any damage, but hard enough that he rubbed the spot where I'd hit him.

"Come with me." He made puppy-dog eyes at me.

"Phil, I'm really not in the mood. I just want this night to be over."

"Was it that bad?"

"Do you want me to start with the water that Olivia slopped all over me at dinner? Or should I just cut right to when Troy elbowed me in the head on the dance floor? Or maybe I'll look fondly back on that disgusting golden retriever kiss he planted on my tonsils. Hmm, it's just so hard to decide what the best part was!"

"Okay, okay, okay." He held up his hands. "I get it. But if you go home now, all you'll have is the bad memories."

I didn't answer.

"Buuu-uuut," he drawled. "If you go to the kick-ass after-party, you'll have fun, and you won't even care about what happened at the dance."

"Seems unlikely."

"Prom is not about the dance, Heart. It's about the rest of the night. Trust me, last year, prom was lame until we got out of here." He jerked his thumb toward the exit. "There is no way the school-sponsored part of the evening can compare to the rest of it."

"Then I'll just spend it with my friends, which is what I should have done in the first place."

"You wound me, Heart. Aren't we friends?"

"That's not what I meant." I flushed with immediate guilt that I'd hurt his feelings. But the truth was, we weren't really friends. I mean, we definitely weren't enemies or anything like that, but apart from our secret *Jeopardy!*-watching sessions, we didn't really do anything together.

"Just come with me. It'll be fun." He tilted his head until he could look me in the eyes. "I'll be gone next year. We'll never have this chance again."

I swear to God, if my brother doesn't end up in sales, something will have gone horribly wrong with the universe. He could sell ice to penguins.

I held off answering as long as I could. I really didn't want to be manipulated, but he'd hit on all the hot spots. The most important of which was that he was leaving. He was right about that. Next year, my little family would be cut down by a third. It would be just me and Dad. Just me, watching *Jeopardy!* alone with my dinner every night.

Then shrieking laughter pulled our attention to the far side of the ballroom. Phil could see what was happening before me with his extra six inches.

"No way," he said.

"What?" I darted and weaved, trying to see around the bodies between the commotion and me. "What?"

"Go Foley!" Phil shouted.

And then I got my first glimpse of pasty white flesh. A senior who went by Foley so ubiquitously that I couldn't even think of his first name was streaking across the dance floor with SENIORS scrawled across his chest in black and orange, and a corsage covering his privates like some kind of fantastic fig leaf.

"Oh my God." Part of me wanted to cover my eyes, but it was way too late for that. The image would be burned into my brain for the rest of my life.

Foley was on the *move*. Dodging around his fully clothed classmates like a running back on the perfect touchdown run. Chaperones were converging from all sides, but Foley had the eye of the tiger. He saw openings where no one else could, spinning out of reach more than once, the red-and-white corsage bobbing and leaping as his penis defied gravity in time with his pace. Just before he darted through one final gap in the chaperones' human net and headed for the exterior doors, I had the hilarious revelation that he must have threaded the wrist strap around his wang to keep the corsage in place so effectively.

I was certain that Foley had just become the stuff of legends.

Cassidy turned to me, mouth agape. "Did that just happen?" she shouted.

"I think it did."

A giggle bubbled up from her mouth, but she made a sad face. "His poor date!"

"That was legendary!" Phil crowed, wrapping his arm around my shoulder again. "Did you see that?"

"Oh, I saw it." I nodded.

"This is the kind of shit that's going to make Blanchard's so epic. You have to come." His eyes were lit up like little flames.

"I don't ever need to see Foley's schlong again, thank you very much."

"Just come with me." He pulled out the puppy-dog face again. "You know you want to."

"I want to hang out with my friends." I held my hands out to indicate the people around us.

Phil thought for a second, then brightened. "Problem solved." He leaned away from me to shout loudly to the No Drama Crew. "You guys should come to Blanchard's house for the after-party!"

Schroeder made a face and gave me a look that said he wasn't thrilled, but Ally and Cassidy perked up.

"Yeah?" Ally asked.

Phil nodded. "Yeah. It's going to be huge."

"I thought we were going to the lake," Schroeder said.

"We have until sunrise," Cassidy said.

"Then you should totally come," Phil said again.

"Come where?" Neel asked, popping into the conversation. Once Ally had explained the invitation to him, he nodded. "Yeah, all right." Neel was always willing to try anything. The more chaotic and social he could be, the happier he was. From the look on Schroeder's face, I knew he was thinking the same thing I was: With Neel and Ally on board, the chances of the No Drama Crew *not* going to Blanchard's party were practically nonexistent.

"Great. Then we'll see you there." He tugged on my wrist. "Come on, Heart, we gotta meet the others back at the limo."

"I'll just go with my friends——" I tried.

"I need your help with Troy. He's about ready to pass out."

"But——"

"Just come with me. We're all going to the same place."

Now I had to decide whether to make a scene, pulling away from my brother like a crabby toddler, or give in and suck it up for one more limo ride. I shot a glance over my shoulder. "I'll see you guys there," I called.

"Hell yeah!" Neel shouted, but I saw the look on Schroeder's face. He was not happy.

Well, that made two of us.

19 Wherein Ryan and I get drafted into an after-party, and I discover a secret fort at the prom

----

TAILS

The only thing missing from Foley's naked run through prom was the old-fashioned sound of a needle scratch and the music going silent. That would have made it perfect. But the DJ just kept the music playing as we all watched the skinny, naked senior lead the chaperones on a merry chase.

I was laughing so hard my stomach hurt up until the moment he turned and gave me a clear view of his bare butt. I flinched and closed my eyes, but it was too late. The image was already a permanent part of my memory. "Oh, gross!"

Cassidy turned to me, mouth agape. "Did that just happen?" she shouted.

"I think it did."

A giggle bubbled up from her mouth, but she made a sad face. "His poor date!"

"Right?" I laughed. Ryan might not dance, but at least he wasn't naked.

"I wonder where his clothes are," Neel said.

"Not on his scrawny ass, that's for sure," Ally said.

"Do you think there will be any more?" Cassidy stood on the toes of her sparkly Chuck Taylors.

"God, I hope not."

"Such a prude," Ally chided.

"This has nothing to do with me being a prude," I said. "No one wanted to see Foley's butt tonight. Much less his junk dressed in flowers."

Cassidy laughed. "I gotta go with my girl on this one," she said, bumping my shoulder. "I did *not* need to see that."

Lisa joined us, slipping her arm through Cassidy's. "So what are you all doing after prom?"

"We're going to the lake," Cass said. The No Drama Prom-a Crew had plans to finish out the night in Neel's family's house. He lived way out in a chichi part of town where the best of the best houses were on a small, private lake. It's good to have two parents who are anesthesiologists, I guess.

"That's just our final destination," Ally said. "We've got the whole night."

"Well, I for one am starving," Neel said.

"Don't your parents have food at their house?"

"I'll never make it that long."

"Neel, it's a twenty-five-minute drive."

"More like forty from here," Neel countered. "I'll probably eat one of you along the way if I have to go that far."

Lisa ignored his zombie-ish growling and gnashing. "You guys should come to Frank Blanchard's house. Marcus wants to go." She rolled her eyes, like letting her boyfriend suggest an activity was sheer madness.

"Blanchard lives near me," Neel said. "Dude's got brick walls around the property, and gates. Have you seen that place? I've always wondered what it was like inside."

"See? It's practically on the way." Lisa clapped her hands once. "It's settled!"

Cassidy shook her head, hands on her hips. "Just like that?"

"Yep." Lisa smiled. "It'll be fun."

"We have to clear it with everybody else," Cassidy said.

"They'll be fine with it." Lisa waved off that suggestion. She was very decisive, my friend.

"I should check with Ryan," I murmured, more to myself than the rest of them, but I also didn't need Lisa overhearing. She was too happy she'd roped some theater geeks into crashing Blanchard's jock fiesta—there was no way she'd want to hear hesitation on my part.

I headed back to the table where Ryan and some other guys were still hanging out. He was laughing as I approached, and I was glad he was having fun, since I'd been unintentionally ignoring him for a while. I told him about Blanchard's party and asked if he wanted to hitch a ride back to his dead car instead. He told me he'd called his parents and they'd arranged to have it towed anyway, so we were at the mercy of whoever was willing to drive us home later.

"So . . . ? Party then?"

He shrugged. "Why not?"

To my left, Schroeder appeared and walked straight to the table where Ryan was sitting. He promptly dropped to his knees, disappearing beneath the long white tablecloth. I did a double take, then went down on one knee to peek under the cloth.

There he was, down on one elbow as he dug through the huge pile of stuff we'd accumulated under the table.

"What are you doing?" I asked.

"Looking for my phone." Schroeder pawed through the abandoned tuxedo jackets and came up with what he was looking for. "Got it!"

I grinned, crawling the rest of the way under the table and letting the cloth drop behind me. "And here I thought you were just pickpocketing everyone."

"I did that earlier." The dim space lit up when he brought his phone to life.

"Did you hear we're going to Frank Blanchard's house? How weird is that?"

In the dim light, I could make out the shape of his body. "What? Why the hell would we do that?"

"Lisa." That was the only explanation I figured was necessary.

"I don't want to go to that guy's house." The screen on the phone timed out, plunging us back into darkness.

"It's apparently not far from Neel's place."

"So, let's just go to Neel's then."

"I'm sure we won't be there long."

"Then let's not go at all." He sounded tense.

I squinted at him, trying to read his face, but we were cloaked in shadows. "What's wrong?"

He sighed and flopped onto his back on the floor. For just a moment, I got the squickies at the thought of what he might be lying in, but I shoved that aside.

"I can't stand Frank Blanchard."

"Why not?"

"Besides the fact that he's the Crown Prince of Douche-burg?"

I snorted. "Yeah, besides that."

"We went to elementary school together. He was a year ahead of me, obviously. And he pretty much hated me."

"Why?"

"Why do sixth graders do anything? I don't know. I just know he went out of his way to make my life miserable."

Because I am at least partially a horrible person, I wanted to laugh. Thankfully, the rest of me seemed to be in charge at that moment, so I managed to sound sympathetic when I said, "I'm sorry."

"Luckily, he seemed to forget who I was by the time we got to high school. Or maybe it was because I ended up taller than him. Who knows? But I don't want to go to his house."

I thought about that for a moment, wiggling my mouth back and forth like a pendulum. It's probably a really good thing we were in the dark; I'm sure I looked like a complete dork. "I have an idea!"

"What?"

"Let's go to his house and do something terrible to him."

He laughed softly. "I don't want to be that guy."

"It doesn't have to be anything permanent or dangerous. It'll just be our little private Screw You."

"Like what?"

"Um . . . we'll short his sheets or something."

Schroeder laughed, this one a much healthier, happier laugh. I was glad I'd apologized to him earlier, hearing his laughter now.

"That's your big revenge plot?" he asked.

"It was just an idea."

"Hmm." He came back up to lean on one elbow, bringing us much closer together again. "It would have to be a really great idea."

"We'll think of something." I could make out his features now that he was nearby, so I wiggled my eyebrows at him, hoping he could see me.

"All right, fine. But you have to help me." A faint scent of mint drifted to me as he spoke.

"On my honor." I crossed my heart, bumping into the now almost completely wilted corsage still clinging to my left boob. I growled at it and sat back to unpin it from my chest. "Do you think Ryan will notice if I leave this thing under here?" I asked.

"You don't like it?" Schroeder asked.

I didn't answer, exactly. "I didn't even know they made corsages without a wrist strap anymore." The pin was hard to unfasten in the dark of our table fort. "I mean, look at this thing. Why would you put flowers on your—" I cut myself off.

This time, I got a full-fledged grin out of him. "Just ditch it," he said.

My heart responded with all kinds of annoying leaps and patters. I really needed to kick Ryan's butt.

20 In which Troy reveals his boxer shorts, and I get beat up by a girl

----

HEADS

The alcohol had finally gotten the best of Troy by the time we got him in the limo, which meant he just sat in his seat with his head lolling backward and his eyes half-closed. I crawled as far into the front of the seating area as possible, wedging myself between Doug and Austin, which wasn't ideal, but I didn't expect either of them to molest me, at least.

"This is gonna be suh-weet!" Austin crowed. "I hear Blanchard's parents moved into the guesthouse for the night, and they're gonna stay completely out of the way. It's going to kick ass."

Frank Blanchard III was our school's answer to Richie Rich. Though I'd never been to his house, I'd heard about it plenty. It had gates. And a guesthouse. And probably a staff of servants.

"How are we supposed to get home from the party?" I wondered aloud, just in case my friends didn't show. It didn't seem impossible that no one had thought of this. "We don't have the limo all night, do we?"

"I left my car at his house earlier." Austin tapped his temple.

While I admired his forethought, I couldn't exactly give him an A+ for his counting skills. There were eight of us. Unless Austin had recently picked up a Lincoln Navigator I wasn't aware of, I had a feeling we weren't all going to fit.

Not that I really had to worry about it, since I was planning on escaping with the No Drama Crew as soon as humanly possible.

Maybe we could just leave as soon as we got there. Go off and do our own thing for the night. Then again, I'd seen the look on Neel's face. I had a feeling he intended to party. Still, a girl could dream. A girl has to dream, or else sink into a self-pitying depression of epic proportions on prom night when she finds herself squeezed between two acquaintances of dubious quality in the back of a limo where she must keep a wary eye on her would-be make-out buddy for the night.

I attempted to fish my phone out of my purse so I could send a text message to Cassidy, imploring them to rescue me from the party. It was almost impossible with all the crap from Aunt Colleen stuffed in there, but I managed it without even having to take the condoms out.

Sometimes, it's the small victories that keep a person going.

Bringing the phone to life, I pulled it close to my chest so no one could read what I was typing. Not that anyone was even paying attention to me.

"Hey, check it out! There's a DVD player in here." Next to me, Doug attempted to pull open a compartment near his hip, but his body was blocking the door. Of course, he thought the solution to this problem was brute force, so he yanked even harder. His elbow thrust back into mine, and my phone shot out of my hands.

Now, you would think in a limo filled with human bodies, half of whom were wearing puffy skirts, the phone would find a soft landing place. But I was in the middle of the prom from hell, so of course, my phone made a beeline for the windows and somehow managed to hit one of the metal strips between them. Although it was too noisy to hear it, I could swear I felt the sound of the touch screen shattering. It didn't explode. It didn't drop a single shard of glass. It just burst into a perfect spiderweb of cracks beaming out from one corner like a work of art.

"Oh no!"

It was Olivia who picked it up and held it out to me. "Here you go." She didn't even seem to notice the screen.

"Crap!" I whispered, cradling my phone like a bird with a broken wing.

"Don't sweat it," Doug said. "You can get it replaced. Just have them switch the chips and you won't lose anything."

I didn't answer. How could I possibly explain to someone like Doug that I didn't exactly have the funds to trot down to the cell phone store and get whatever the latest, greatest model was? I was on my dad's business plan, and they don't even get new phones every two years like a regular plan. I clicked the power button and the screen lit up, but I was too afraid to touch the shattered screen to write any messages.

So, I gently tucked it back into my purse, feeling terribly sorry for myself and trying not to cry. And when a bottle of cake-flavored vodka made the rounds through the back of the car, I gave in and took a drink. It smelled kind of delicious anyway, and I figured I deserved a little something after everything I'd been through that night. Just enough to get me to the party, and then I'd sneak away from all these people with my stupid, useless phone and escape from this miserable night.

The vodka was easier to drink than I'd expected. It actually wasn't even half bad. It might have even been delicious for real if it were cold. It was better than anything else they'd offered up for the night, that was for sure, so when it came around for a second time, I let a larger swig trickle down my throat.

Randi grinned at me. "So yummy, right?"

I smothered a cough before answering. "Not bad."

"It's really good in chocolate milk," she said.

In a weird way, I could almost picture that, but the thought of milk mixing in my stomach with all that harsh alcohol also made me a little pukey. It didn't take long to get past it, though, when the drink started to kick in. Everyone in the limo suddenly seemed a little farther away, and my nerves seemed to drift off to slumber land inside my body. Was this why they drank? To detach from the real world a little bit? Were their in-crowd lives so painful they had to live them with a blur to take the edge off?

Heavy thoughts. Heavier than I wanted at the moment.

Also, apparently heavier than my head could support.

Letting it drop back onto the seat like Troy was doing, I let my mind wander over the events of the evening. Suddenly, my dress ripping didn't seem quite so traumatic. More . . . hilarious. And getting a bath in the water from the center-piece seemed like a funny story I'd probably tell for the rest of my life. Yeah, none of that was so bad at all.

Dancing with my friends had been fun. Especially when Schroeder took me out on the floor for some tricks and spins. That had been really, really fun. And he looked so handsome in his tux.

Handsome. That was a weird word. I formed the letters with my mouth, not sure if anyone would hear me over the music pumping from the speakers. Olivia was trying to dance to the beat, but her prom queen crown kept droop-ing. I smiled, watching her swoop it back into place over and over again. I wanted to tell her to just take it off, but then again, I'd never had a crown, so maybe she didn't want to take it off. Maybe it felt awesome.

"Can I try on your crown?" I asked, but she didn't hear me.

It seemed like too much effort to try again, especially when I could just sit back and let the light show running along the ceiling of the limo play across my retinas. There should be more light shows in life, I decided. Like, at the dentist. I would stare at the ceiling all day if only my dentist had a laser light show.

The limo also had a miniature disco ball, I noticed. And suddenly, I needed to see it in action.

"Let's turn on the disco ball," I said, pointing to it.

"What?" Doug asked.

"Disco ball. We should turn it on."

He looked at me with sudden appreciation. "We *should* turn it on." He twisted around and knocked on the smoked-glass divider between us and the driver, demanding the disco ball start spinning. I couldn't tell if the driver ever lowered the glass, but suddenly the little mirrored ball came to life, spraying the interior with reflected light.

"Woo!" Olivia and Randi squealed, and started dancing more. Randi's smaller princess crown slipped off her head almost immediately, and right into Doug's lap. I grabbed it and planted it on my own head. It pushed one of my pin curls into my eye, but I didn't care.

"How do I look?" I asked everyone and no one.

"Yo, Phil! I think your sister's drunk!" Doug shouted.

Phil looked at me in surprise. "Seriously?"

"I'm not drunk." Wiping my suddenly itchy nose with gusto, I looked around the limo. "Where'd that cake stuff go?"

"I think you *are* drunk," Phil said, grinning.

"I don't think that's your think to think," I told him, eyebrows lifting. I attempted to tilt my head back and look haughty.

He laughed, teasing. "Somebody needs to cut you off."

"You're not the boss of me."

"Leave her alone." Randi butted into the conversation. "She's having fun."

"Yeah. I'm having fun," I echoed.

"It's about damn time. But I'm still not taking responsibility if you puke," Phil warned me.

"She's not going to puke."

"I'm not going to puke," I repeated. Man, Randi had never made so much sense before.

"Whatever." Phil rolled his eyes, so I stuck my tongue out. It was really only the start of what he deserved after saddling me with his drunk, tongue-happy buddy for the night.

Leaning back into the seat, I let my eyelids hover just above shut and went back to contemplating life, the universe, and everything. But mostly the prom. I thought back to Cassidy's question about how I'd pictured my prom night. When she'd set up the imaginary last dance, and how I'd tried to look up at my date's face. At least now I knew it wasn't Troy. I shuddered, which struck me funny for some reason, and I smiled to myself. Now that I thought about it, I realized I hadn't danced with anyone at the end of the prom. Well, okay, I'd been dancing in a big group, but there was no final-scene-in-the-romantic-movie moment. My nine-year-old self would be so disappointed.

I giggled. Out loud, I think. The only person I'd even come close to that kind of moment with was Schroeder.

Huh.

I guess it sort of made sense. He was such a good dancer, after all. We'd been partnered in last year's musical, and I remember thinking that he'd actually make fairly decent crush material. But I can hardly be held responsible for such irrational thoughts. How is a girl supposed to resist someone who can twirl her around like Fred Astaire? She can't, that's how.

It wasn't just the dancing, though. I knew that. That would be a new low in crush factor for me. Although my endless lust for Captain Jack Sparrow wasn't based on a whole lot more. Not to mention Captain Jack was a raging alcoholic.

Ah, pirates . . . can't live with 'em, can't live without 'em.

I shook my head, trying to rattle my thoughts into

some kind of alignment, but it wasn't working. They were spinning as fast as the reflections from the disco ball.

I hiccuped, and discovered that cake vodka doesn't taste quite as good on the way up. I'd have to warn my friends about that once I found them at that party.

If I found them.

They had to come.

They were coming. I knew they were. Although Schroeder hadn't looked too happy about the whole thing.

Schroeder, Schroeder, Schroeder. Chase. I struggled to think of him by his real name. It wasn't a bad name. Kind of nice actually. Maybe even a little sexy? I'd called him Schroeder for so long, though, it was hard not to. Schroeder was not a nice name. It definitely wasn't sexy.

Of course, based on the look he'd given me as I was leaving, I didn't have to worry about what his name was. He'd looked mad. Which was so weird.

Suddenly, Troy sat bolt upright, eyes going wider than I'd seen them all night.

"Aw, shit!" Austin seemed to know what the move meant, and turned to pound on the glass divider behind the driver. "Pull over!" he shouted. "Pull over!"

"Ew! Ew! Ew!" Randi shrieked, scrambling away from Troy and practically onto Doug's lap.

"What?" I demanded, confused.

"He's gonna hurl!" Randi squealed.

Adrenaline brought me completely out of my stupor in an instant. I looked around for anything that could serve as a barf bucket while Austin continued to pound on the divider. Finally the limo slowed and pulled toward the curb. Just in time, too. Phil threw open the door at the last second, and Troy got one foot out onto the street before he puked.

It was an epic spew. One for the history books. I squeezed my eyes shut and tried to cover my ears, but it was almost impossible to move with Randi half on top of me. The other girls shoved their way toward my end of the limo, too, making it hard to breathe.

"You okay, man?" I heard Phil ask, though I couldn't see anything but sparkles, hair, and skirts.

There were a few more heaving sounds that made my stomach lurch, and then Troy's voice said, "Yeah. I'm good."

"That was fuckin' nasty, bro," Phil said.

On top of me, the girls relaxed a little bit, and I caught some fresh air as their weight moved away.

"Does anyone have any water?" Randi asked. "If I'm going to sit next to him again, he's going to need to rinse his mouth. I can't sit next to vomit breath."

"Eww!" Olivia said.

"There's a water up here if you'll fucking *move!*" Doug snapped, pushing at Randi. She did a tongue click and gave him a nasty expression as she slid away, leaving Doug free to reach over and grab a small water bottle from the limo's own supply.

Austin pounded on the divider again and shouted, "Can you pull forward a little?"

The limo lurched five feet ahead, leaving Troy's puke puddle behind us, and Doug thrust the water bottle at Troy, who was now sitting on the floor of the limo with his feet hanging out.

"Rinse your mouth out and make sure you didn't get any on your shoes," Randi said sharply. I could picture her being the kind of mom who snaps at her kids in a restaurant if they spill a drop.

Troy got out to stand in the gutter, his legs wobbling. "I think I got some on my pants," he said.

Dear God, whatever I did to offend you, I'm deeply sorry. Please accept my apology and deliver me from this prom-themed purgatory.

Olivia sneered at the door. "He is not coming back in here if there is puke on his pants."

"Calm down, Liv," Phil said. "It's not like you've never

barfed on your pants before."

"I have *not!*" Olivia barked. "And he is not coming in here like that."

"What's he supposed to do, babe?" Austin asked.

"He can walk for all I care."

My heart hurt, listening to them snipe at each other. I wanted to help Troy, but at the same time, I really didn't want to risk another fish-tongue episode.

"Hey, Troy!" Doug called. "Liv wants you to take your pants off!"

"Wha—?" Troy bent slightly to look through the door at us. His eyes were almost crossing, he was so out of it.

"Take. Your. Pants. Off," Doug repeated.

Troy shrugged, and the next thing I knew, he was undoing the fasteners on his tux pants.

"Oh my God!" I gasped. I wanted to cover my eyes, I really did.

Doug and Phil were cackling like morons, and Olivia was shrilling at Troy not to move another muscle. The noise must have been too much for Troy to comprehend, though, because his pants hit the ground. Turns out, his boxer shorts were white with tigers on them. You know, to match my corsage.

"Go Tigers!" Phil cheered.

Checking first to see if anyone was looking, I slipped my corsage off my wrist and set it on the window ledge. That was enough of that.

"Oh my freaking God, would you pull your pants up?" Randi yelled.

He did. And then he did the last thing I would have ever predicted. He bellowed, "AMY!" at the top of his lungs and took off running.

We all watched in stunned confusion as Troy, pants still held up by both hands and undone at the fly, ran across four lanes of traffic toward the bank on the other side of the street. Brakes squealed, horns honked, and one car swerved so hard it ended up on the curb.

"What the fuck . . . ?" Doug said what we were all thinking.

Phil, being closest to the door, got out for a better look, while Doug popped up through the sunroof. Tara cupped her hands against the privacy glass, peering out into the dark night.

"Oh shit, that *is* Amy," she muttered.

I got free of my seat and crawled over to kneel beside Tara and look for myself.

Sure enough, Amy and her mystery date were in the parking lot of the bank. It looked like one of them had just come from the ATM at the front of the building. Troy was standing between them, fumbling to close the clasp on his pants.

Phil swung back into the limo with a grin and looked straight at Doug. "Tell the driver to head over there."

Doug did, and the driver complied, waiting for a break in traffic to make his way across the boulevard to the parking lot where Amy was now in between Troy and her mystery date, with her arms outstretched like she was trying to keep them apart.

Phil rubbed his hands together, laughing gleefully. "Ooh-hoo-hoo! Looks like a fight to me!"

"Fight! Fight! Fight!" Doug chanted with a fist punching the air.

"You guys better get in there and break it up," Tara warned them. "Troy looks like he wants to kill that guy."

The shouting match was already in progress by the time Phil opened the door.

"—are you, anyway?"

"Why don't you just back the fuck off, buddy?"

"Fuck you!"

"Go!" Tara waved the guys toward the door. Austin and Doug didn't need any coaxing to obey. I hadn't seen them this excited all night.

"You need your little friends to back you up, tough guy?"

"Rob, stop!" That was Amy, which led me to believe the mystery date's name was Rob.

"I don't need anybody!" And that was when Troy bum-rushed Rob, fist flying through the air.

I winced, but there was no sound of impact. I opened my eyes cautiously to find Troy on his knees behind the empty space where Rob had been standing. Doug had Rob in a bear hug from behind, while Phil was trying to get Troy to his feet.

I could barely keep track of who was shouting and who the aggressor was at any given time, but suddenly, they were all in a scuffle, with Amy screaming at them to stop. Tara got out, her dress shimmering like a diamond in the overhead light of the parking lot. She grabbed Phil by the elbow and hauled him back with such unexpected force that he fell on his butt.

"Stop it! All of you!" Tara commanded. She wasn't shouting, but somehow her voice carried through all the noise, and everyone went still. "What is wrong with you people?" she said, glaring at each of them in turn.

"Tell them, Amy! Tell 'em you don't want to see him anymore!" Rob shouted. From my position against the window, I could see that his nose was bleeding.

"Amy, no!" Troy moaned.

"Oh, now you're upset?" Amy snapped. "You expect me to believe you want me back? I *saw* you kissing that girl at prom—"

"No, Amy. I'm sorry! No!" Troy was on the verge of tears.

So I made a stupid decision. I scrambled out of the limo and rushed to the edge of the gathered crowd. "We're not together!" I said to Amy, pointing between Troy and me. "It was just a mistake—"

But she didn't let me finish talking. She ran at me, outstretched hands slamming into my shoulders so hard I was on my ass before I had even processed her first move. My teeth rattled together, and I fell back on my elbows.

It took me a second to realize Amy was screaming at me. ". . . take my boyfriend from me? I'll mess you up!"

Somebody caught her around the waist, hauling her back before she could get her hands on me again, and then Randi was behind me, helping me sit up.

"Are you okay?" she gasped.

"I don't—" I couldn't even think of words to speak. I had never been so shocked in my life.

"Everybody just needs to calm down!" Tara said in her

crowd-control voice again.

I blinked, turning to look at Randi like she might be able to explain how exactly I had landed on my ass in the middle of a parking lot.

She tugged on my elbow. "Come on, get up."

"What happened?" I asked, dazed.

"Amy's a psycho bitch, that's what happened," Randi said, loud enough to get Amy fighting against Doug's tight hold on her again.

"You're the bitch, *Randi*," she snarled.

I looked up at the sky briefly, unable to find any stars through the glare of the lights.

Really, God? Really? Not even a little deliverance?

"Heart, are you all right?" Troy slurred.

"Heart? Are you fucking kidding me?" Amy laughed.

That narrowed my focus at last, and I looked straight at her. "I didn't even want to be here," I said.

"What?" she hissed.

"Never mind. You guys deserve each other." I turned and made my way to the limo, trying not to give her the satisfaction of watching me limp, even though my tailbone rang with pain at each step.

Crawling carefully back into the car, I winced as I sat on the seat. Olivia was the only person still in the car. She was scanning her cell phone, with her legs crossed and one foot bouncing idly.

I sucked air through my teeth as I scooted down the long bench toward the spot where I'd been sitting before. Olivia looked over the top of her phone at me.

"Are they done yet?" she asked.

"I don't know." I winced.

"What's wrong with you?"

"I got knocked down."

She shook her head in disgust. "That's why I don't get involved. It's not worth it."

"Yeah, well, maybe you could have told me that before I went out there."

Olivia looked at me again, one perfect eyebrow lifting slightly. "You in pain?" she asked.

"Yeah, kind of."

She lowered her phone enough to reach over and grab the bottle of cake-flavored vodka again. "Have some more. It'll help."

So I did.

21 Wherein condiments become condom-ents, and I kiss Ryan

TAILS

The drive-through line for Taco Bell was at least ten cars deep. Pat, once again behind the wheel of the day-care-slash-serial-killer van, made a sharp right and veered into a parking space at the last minute, tossing me into Ryan. "My need for tacos is too great to wait in this line!" Pat held one finger aloft. "We're going in!"

Not surprisingly, Neel was the first one out of the van. He'd been going on about how hungry he was since before the dance had even ended. Everyone unloaded and headed for the restaurant's door. Our gear caught the attention of a few people in line, and we got honked at. Cassidy curtsied deeply in the beam of someone's headlights, fanning her face and demurring like she'd been given a third curtain call.

God, I love my friends.

When the inner doors opened, the smell of half-assed fast-food Mexican wafted at me, and suddenly I was starving. This was far from gourmet eating, but when the stomach craves the Bell, there is no cure but the Bell itself. I happily hopped into line behind Dan, already calculating how many soft tacos it would take to satisfy my needs.

Ryan slid his hands along the wooden railings meant to herd us toward the register in a zigzag pattern. Hoisting himself up like a gymnast on the parallel bars, he leaned ominously toward me for a second and I squealed, anticipating him falling on me. But apparently, not everyone is as physically inept as I am, so he just righted himself and landed on his feet.

"You're gonna break your neck." I swatted him on the shoulder with my overloaded clutch purse and the clasp burst open, spewing the contents out like a party popper. "Oh no!" I made a fumbling grab for my cell phone, but it took a nosedive and slammed into the tile floor on one corner like a spiked football.

Everyone held their breath as we waited for the telltale sound of a shattered screen, and we weren't disappointed. The tiny *pop!* made my blood run cold. Several people

gasped in unison, which was almost funny, even considering the circumstance.

Already I could see the back of the phone was cracked
like a windshield after a rock bounces off at high speed. I
sucked in some air and squatted down to get it, feeling the
strain across my duct-tape dress patch. When I turned it
over, the front screen was totally unharmed.

"Woo-hoo!" I held it up, victorious, and everyone
cheered.

"It's a prom miracle!" Neel declared.

"Nice." Ryan smiled at him.

"Oh my God, I am so happy right now." I held up my
hands to Neel and Ryan, who happened to be the closest,
and they pulled me to my feet. "I love you, sweet phone." I
planted a kiss on the unbroken screen, leaving behind a lip
print, sticky with my freshly applied gloss.

"Nice move, genius." Neel rolled his eyes.

"Whatever, I don't even care." I clutched my phone to
my chest and smiled at them all.

"Um, what about the rest of your crap?" Ally bent
down to pick up the roll of Rolaids that had landed near
her foot. "You'll definitely want these after eating at Taco
Hell."

"I just need my money. I don't really care about the

rest." In fact, I considered the rest of Aunt Colleen's treats to be an appropriate offering to the gods of cell phones and eighty-nine-cent tacos.

Everyone searched the area around the railed-in line, calling out as they each discovered small bits of my life. But the vintage silver cigarette case where I'd tucked my driver's license and a small amount of cash was nowhere to be found.

"Ooh, gum!" Cassidy said. "Is this yours?"

"Yeah, probably, but I can't guarantee it."

"Can I have it?"

"Whatever. Just look for the silver case."

"Bandages?" Schroeder asked.

"Those were mine, too," I answered. "I guess I could take them back."

He held them out to me from the other side of the wooden corral we were queued up in. I smiled at him as I took them back, and he returned a smile of his own.

"Money!" Dan shouted, and I leaped to my feet to see, but he was only holding up a quarter.

"Keep looking," I said, as I dropped back to a squat. All around me, I saw nothing but dirty brown tiles. Had I been pickpocketed in the middle of the dance? Where the hell was my silver case? "Shoot," I muttered as the first traces of panic surfed through my veins. "Shoot, shoot, damn it!"

"Is this it?" Ryan called, holding up the small metal box.

"Yes!" I jumped up and ran at him, throwing my arms around his neck and laying a big, smacky kiss on his lips. "Oh my God, you have no idea how happy I am right now!"

"Who's the greatest prom date in the world?" he asked, tucking me under his arm to hold the case out to me.

"Obviously you!" I plucked it from his fingertips and flicked it open with a practiced move to reveal undisturbed contents. "Huzzah! It's all here!" I grabbed his chin and planted another kiss on his cheek, leaving behind yet another lip print.

"Does that mean you're buying me a taco?" Ryan winked at me.

"I'll even throw in a burrito."

With my crisis averted, Neel took the opportunity to cut past us in line and be the first to order. He was a man with a plan, cash already in hand to make the transaction. I guess he wasn't kidding about being ready to go cannibal on us if he didn't get some chow soon. As soon as he had his change, he slid down to the pickup end of the counter and went for the packets of sauce.

No sooner had I turned my attention back to the menu than a bellow of laughter brought my eyes to Neel again. "Oh man!" he cackled. "Somebody's going to be very disappointed when they bust out a packet of mild sauce in bed later!" He held up an all-too-familiar strip of three pleasure-shaped condoms, and my face burst into flames.

"Eww! Who does that?" Ally demanded. "Put them down! There's probably herpes all over them."

"Ah God, Ally, you had to go there?" Neel moaned. "Now how am I supposed to enjoy my chalupa?"

"Stop spazzing, they're mine." I held out my hand, but all I got in return was silence and the confused stares of seven of my dearest friends.

"*Yours?*" Ally demanded.

"Yes," Ryan said right away. "For all the hot sex we're going to have later."

I tried to squelch the laughter bubbling up from my chest, but it was impossible, and it burst out of my mouth in an unladylike donkey bray. I grinned at Ryan and emphasized my empty hand for Neel. "Can I have them, please?"

Neel looked at me, looked at Ryan, back to me, to the condoms, and back to Ryan again before stretching out his arm to set the strip in my hand. He screwed up his whole face into an expression of disbelief. "There you go. You kids enjoy yourselves."

"Thank you." I tucked them into my purse, distinctly aware that the ambient noise of the group was at near zero. Looking at Cassidy's and Ally's faces made me roll my eyes, laughing. "Would you guys relax? My dumb aunt gave them to me along with all the other crap that went all over creation."

Cassidy's face dissolved into understanding. All she was missing was the cartoon lightbulb over her head. "I should have known Colleen was involved."

"I know, right?" I shook my head.

Cassidy nudged Ally in the back, and she took her place at the cash register to order. Everyone else shuffled up behind her, giving me a clear view of Schroeder, who was staring at me with disappointment. As soon as he saw me looking, he shifted his eyes to the menu board, but his posture remained stiff.

I'd never seen him go prudish on anyone before, so it was hard to imagine he was giving me the cold shoulder over condoms I had no intention of using, but the guy was being downright weird tonight. Or maybe I was being oversensitive because of Ryan's theory. No. It didn't seem possible that it was completely in my head—I'd experienced subtler temperature changes in the shower after Phil flushed the toilet in the other bathroom.

Seemed like maybe it was time to call him out on the mood swings. And this time I wasn't going to apologize like Ryan had made me do before. I considered my options and decided to bide my time until we got to the party, and then I'd corner him. And with a plan in place, I was free to enjoy my disgusting but somehow satisfying tacos. With condom-free mild sauce.

22 In which Troy loses consciousness, and I am kidnapped by jocks

----

HEADS

I had become a hostage.

After the parking lot fight, Amy and the infamous Rob left with squealing tires and shouted obscenities, while my brother and his friends crawled back into the limo, all hopped up on post-fight adrenaline.

Apparently, fighting works up an appetite, because Doug declared he was going to starve to death, and the others were quick to agree. None of the other girls seemed to care one way or another, and my attempts to protest that we were supposed to meet the No Drama Crew at Blanchard's house fell on deaf ears.

The limo driver aimed the stretch SUV in the complete opposite direction I wanted to go, and someone cranked the music back up. Troy, his pants now wet from the knees down thanks to Randi dumping several bottles of water on him before allowing him entrance to the limo, took three long swigs from the latest bottle of whatever it was they were drinking and let out a terrifying belch just before his eyes rolled up in his head and he passed out.

"Is he okay?" I asked Austin, who was next to me again.

He didn't look away from his attempts to slip his fingers under the top of Olivia's dress but said, "He's fine."

"Great." I sighed. My head was still swimming with vodka-y fuzziness, but it wasn't the pleasant, dreamy feeling I'd had earlier. Now I couldn't be sure if the limo was turning corners, or if that was just going on in my own head. I scrounged for my clutch, almost getting kicked in the head by Randi, who was a lot more receptive to Doug's advances than Olivia was to Austin's.

I had to get out of here.

The only positive about the gropefests going on to either side of me was that they were taking up less room glommed together like that. So I could open my purse and gingerly fish out my broken cell phone. The screen was already alive with a handful of text messages.

Cassidy: *Emergency Taco Bell run, be there in a few.*

Cassidy: *Do you want some T-Bell?*

Cassidy: *Hel-lo <poke>*

Kim: *U missed yr chance. Left T-Bell.*

Cassidy: *Where R U?*

Cassidy: *Srsly. Where R U?*

I typed in a quick reply. *Troy took his pants off. Parking lot fight. I've been kidnapped. Help!*

The reply came almost immediately. Cassidy: *OMG R U OK? Where R U?*

I typed in a longer version, but it was hard to concentrate with the amateur pornography going on to my right. I wasn't sure how well I explained everything.

Cassidy: *R U coming???*

Me: *Yes. Soon.*

Me: *I hope.*

Lisa: *Get out of the limo. Marcus will come get you.*

Me: *We're still driving.*

Lisa: *As soon as you stop.*

Cassidy: *Screw that! Jump!!!!*

Me: *I AM NOT JUMPING OUT OF A MOVING CAR!*

The limo turned into the parking lot of a diner, and my heart sank.

"I thought we'd be going to a drive-through or something," I said, but no one was paying any attention to me.

"Yo, Rafferty!" Phil elbowed Troy to wake him,

but he didn't move. Phil shrugged and opened the door. "Let's go."

Doug waved off the command. "Go 'head," he muttered.

I scooted out of the way just as Randi swung her leg over Doug's lap to straddle him. And even though my butt was still a little sore from getting shoved to the ground, I moved. Fast. I did *not* want to be present for whatever came next. I caught a look at Troy on my way to the door, but he wasn't moving. Just breathing heavily through his mouth and drooling slightly.

Audrey Hepburn would never put up with this crap.

I ran a few steps to catch up with Phil and poked him in the shoulder. "This is going to take too long. Can't we just go to the party?"

"I'm hungry."

"Phil, my friends are waiting for me."

He shrugged. "You should have gone with them."

I stopped walking, my fingers stretching into very angry jazz hands, then curling into fists. Anger rattled through me, making my stomach cramp and my muscles quiver with tension.

Tara patted me once on the shoulder as she swept past. "Should have had another drink when you had the chance."

She looked back at me. "Makes it easier, trust me."

Rock. Hard place. Me.

I couldn't go back to the limo, or who knew what I'd have to see from the Randi and Doug show. And I didn't want to go into the diner. What I wanted to do was hit Phil over the head with my purse. Or a baseball bat.

Getting my shattered phone back out, I sent an SOS to Lisa, begging for a pickup. It took her way too long to get back to me, and frustrated tears were beginning to gather on my lashes and make my nose run.

Lisa: *I can't find Marcus. Hold on.*

Just then, the limo door opened and Randi came out looking pissed. She gave her dress a yank to straighten it and stalked toward the diner without a backward glance. Doug came out a few minutes later looking annoyed, but he was in no hurry as he fastened his pants and smoothed his hair. He spotted me leaning against a parked car near the entrance. "What's wrong with you?" It didn't sound like concern, or even curiosity. More like irritation.

I stared at him. "Absolutely nothing."

"Whatever." He passed me by and disappeared into the diner, and I went back to the limo.

I considered knocking on the passenger door and asking the driver if I could sit with him, but I wasn't really in the mood for small talk. So I climbed into the backseat again, carefully avoiding any contact with Troy for fear of waking him.

Then, all by myself, and feeling about as pathetic as I've ever felt in my life, I sat in the corner and helped myself to a few more sips of the cake-flavored vodka. It was either that or go on a homicidal rampage with a spoon.

Note to self: find a spoon. Just in case.

23 Wherein I learn what a spinet is, and that Ryan is wise

TAILS

My plan to confront Schroeder post–Taco Bell was all well and good, except that I couldn't seem to find him anywhere. I knew he'd come into Blanchard's house with us. I'd walked in right behind him, in fact, but then it was like I'd blinked and he'd been sucked through a rip in reality to another dimension. There was no trace of the boy, no matter where I looked.

On my quest, I stumbled across a lot of strange sights. Some sweet, like the couple who didn't know I could see them when he stole a kiss from her and she smiled and leaned her forehead against his. Some funny, like the two guys doing an impressive rendition of a Lady Gaga dance. Some depressing, like the girl crying on the basement stairs. And some downright disturbing, like my brother lying on a Ping-Pong table in the garage with the business end of a funnel in his mouth and someone I didn't know cracking a beer over the other end.

No one seemed to know where Schroeder was. My feet ached as I climbed the stairs to the second floor for the third time. I was fairly convinced he was just avoiding me at this point, but I couldn't seem to stop my body from moving through room after room of the ridiculously huge Blanchard house. Mansion. Whatever.

A lot of the second floor rooms' doors were closed, and I was sure at least a few of them were concealing scenes between couples I didn't want any part of. I felt like a complete creep as I paused outside each closed door, listening for any sign of life inside that wasn't of the X-rated variety. Finally, outside a set of double doors at the end of the hall, I heard the faint sound of classical music inside.

I took a risk, easing open the doors slowly and peeping through the crack to make sure I wasn't going to disturb anyone.

Jackpot.

There was Schroeder, sitting at a small upright piano under a wide mullioned window.

"Hey," I said softly, approaching at an angle so he would see me.

"Hi." He didn't look back, but his fingers rose from the keys. They danced along the surface of the ivory for a moment before settling into a new position. The fingers of his right hand went to work, picking out the opening notes to "Für Elise." I pressed my own fingertips against my breastbone, as instant feelings of wistfulness stirred at the sound.

His left hand joined the tune, and for a long moment I simply watched him play. I'd had my share of piano lessons as a kid, but I'd never come close to this level. I'd like to blame my small hands, but the truth was I just wasn't interested enough in the instrument.

Watching Schroeder play made me wish I'd stuck with it.

When he got to the busier bridge of the song, he trailed off, turning slightly to look at me. "Did you need something?"

"I like listening to you play," I said. "You're Schroeder, after all."

"Mmm." He put his hands in his lap. "I probably shouldn't be in here anyway."

"No one seems to care." I shrugged. "And frankly, I'm

surprised they only have this little piano. Seems like the sort of place that should have one of those shiny grand pianos."

"This is just a spinet," he said, as if that meant something to me. "I think this is a practice room for all the other instruments." He gestured vaguely to a pair of music stands and a violin case on the floor. "The grand piano is downstairs. Didn't you see it?"

"Oh." I thought back to my multiple trips through the living room. He was right; there was exactly the glossy, showpiece instrument I would have imagined, sitting in a small alcove surrounded by windows. "Well. Must be nice to be two-piano rich."

He smiled slightly. "No kidding."

I pursed my lips, waiting for him to say more, but nothing came. "What's your deal tonight?"

"I already told you, I don't like Frank Blanchard."

"Not about that. What's your deal with me tonight?"

He looked in my eyes. "I don't have a deal with you."

"You're acting like you do."

"If you say so." He turned back to the piano and carefully lowered the lid over the keys. I felt like he was closing the lid on our conversation, and frankly, it pissed me off.

"I do say so. One minute we're dancing and having a

good time, the next you won't even let me be in the group pictures."

His body went still, though I still couldn't see his face.

"I'm right, aren't I? You're pissed at me."

"No," he said after a long moment.

I marched up to the piano bench and stared at the side of his head until he couldn't stand it anymore and looked at me. "Then why are you being so horrible? I apologized for ditching out on the No Drama thing already and you said we were cool, but you're not acting like we're cool."

"You kissed Ryan."

"What?" I took a step back, confused for a moment, before I remembered how I'd gone all over-the-top when Ryan had found my wallet at Taco Bell.

"I was right there. Everybody was."

"So? I was just happy he found my ID and my money."

He shook his head. "All this time you've been saying you don't date, not anybody, no matter what, and suddenly that's all out the door."

"What?" I squinted at him in confusion. "It wasn't like that. It was nothing—"

"Whatever, I can take a hint."

"What are you talking about?"

"I'm just saying if you didn't want to go out with

someone, all you had to do was say no. You didn't have to make up some stupid rule to—what? Make yourself feel better?"

"Schroeder, I am not going out with Ryan. Trust me. And what do you care, anyway?"

He got up from the piano bench with a frustrated growl. "I don't." But then his face scrunched up, and he pressed his fists into his temples. "I like you, okay? I wanted to ask you to prom, but I didn't because of your stupid rule, but you just—you show up with Ryan, and . . ." He splayed his fingers wide and brought his hands down to his sides. "You know what? Forget it. I don't even want to talk about it."

My heart was in my throat, and my nerves were jangling as he stalked toward the double doors. I felt like I'd just been dropped in the middle of a game where I didn't know any of the rules and no one would stop playing long enough to tell me. "Wait! You don't understand—Schroeder, wait!"

He wheeled around impatiently. "What?"

"I'm not dating Ryan."

"Okay."

"I'm not!"

"I said okay," he repeated.

"I just wanted to make sure you knew that."

He sighed. "Then why'd you go to prom with him?"

"Because he asked me!" I shouted.

"So that's all it takes to violate the big No Dating rule? Pretty weak rule."

"Trust me, this is so not a date." I shook my head.

"You sure he knows that?"

"Oh my God, yes."

"You really sure? I tend to get a little confused about that myself when the girls I ask out kiss me in front of a bunch of people."

"Schroeder. Trust me." I held up both hands. "Ryan is *not* interested in me."

"You can't know that."

"I do." Trying to make eye contact was proving pointless. How was I supposed to will him to read my mind when he wouldn't look at me? I needed him to guess Ryan's secret. It wouldn't be me telling if he guessed, right?

"So why would he even ask you?"

"We're friends!" I shouted.

"You just better hope you're right, 'cause if you're not . . ." He shook his head slowly.

"Then what?" I demanded, hands on hips.

He shrugged. "I guess that would make you kind of heartless, wouldn't it?"

"You know, I've had it with you." I stepped closer, whispering loudly in his face. "You've been so rude to me, and I didn't even do anything wrong." I pointed my finger in front of his nose before he could protest. "Uh-uh. I had *no idea* how you felt about me. None. And you know whose fault that is? Yours. If you wanted to ask me to prom, you should have frigging asked me. You don't get to whine about it just because somebody else had the balls to do what you didn't. I'm done apologizing to you." I poked him in the chest. "I didn't do anything wrong. Get over yourself."

Shaking and on the verge of tears—God, I hate confronting people—I turned my back on him.

He didn't reach for me. He didn't even say a word. Just walked away.

There, I told myself. You did what you needed to do.

So why did I feel so awful?

HEADS

I don't know how long I sat there, listening to the driver's music choices—country, as it turned out—but I'd fully rebuilt my buzz by the time they all came back.

"All right," Doug crowed as Phil shut the door behind him. "Let's get to Blanchard's already!"

I thought it was very big of me not to hit him in the head with the bottle of vodka I was still holding.

They all seemed quite restored by their late-night snack at the diner, chattering and laughing all the way. Even sourpuss Olivia was smiling now and then, and she didn't try to stop Austin when he groped her. Across from me, Troy continued to snooze. I actually envied him. So, I leaned back into my seat and closed my eyes.

I'll think about all this tomorrow. At Tara.

I didn't open my eyes until the limo pulled to a stop at Frank Blanchard's house. Or should I say mansion? I tried not to go completely slack-jawed when I stepped out onto the long driveway, but I'm not sure how successful I was. The place was huge. The word that came to mind was château. Stone block walls, high pointy roofs over tall windows. Lights shone up from the ground at the exterior walls and around some of the trees on the sloping lawn.

"Ho-ly shhhh . . ." I pressed my lips closed before Phil and his band of Merry Jocks could catch me gawking.

"About fucking time," Randi groused as she got out of the limo. "I gotta pee so bad." She scurried toward the house, leaving everyone else behind.

"Come on, let's go around the back. I'm sure everyone's outside anyway," Tara announced.

"Hang on, we gotta get Troy outta there." Phil indicated the limo.

"Driver's done," Doug agreed. "We gotta find somewhere to dump Troy."

Olivia sighed. "Just take him in the house and meet us by the pool."

I had precisely zero clue where to go. Where would my friends be? I decided the safer option was sticking with the girls as they headed around the side of the house. Tara had said everyone would be in the backyard, and I really didn't want to be in the splash zone if Troy came to and gave a repeat performance of his world-record-setting barf routine.

Tara and Olivia were already walking away when Tara turned back to look at me. "Are you coming, Heart?"

I jogged a few steps to catch up with them, but that was a colossal mistake. The ground seemed to heave under my feet, and I had to throw both hands out to steady myself. "Whoa!"

"You okay?" Tara asked.

I nodded, blinking hard.

"Oh, you're drunk, aren't you?" Tara cooed.

"Maybe."

They giggled together. "Aww, they're so cute when they're young like this." Olivia made an isn't-she-adorable face.

I showed great personal strength and integrity by not kicking her.

"I'm gonna look for my friends," I said instead, walking a little faster to put some ground between them and me. I had reached my limit.

About five hours ago.

I spotted Cassidy first, jumping on one of those humongous trampolines. It was in a shadowy part of the yard, but Cass's blond hair and pink dress were unmistakable, catching the light every time she reached the top of her jump. Plus, she was laughing and talking the whole time, so it was kind of hard to miss her.

"Wait!" she was calling down to whoever was on the far side of the trampoline. "Wait! I'm totally gonna do it this time, I swear!"

"Yeah, right!" Neel said from the shadows. "You can't do it."

"Cass!" I shouted, jogging to the trampoline.

She spun to face me, and her face lit up. "Heart! Oh my God, you're alive!" Flipping her legs out in front of her, she bounced on her butt a few times to kill her momentum and scrambled off the edge of the jumping surface before throwing her arms around me.

"Oh my God! Where have you been? We were so worried about you!"

"Yeah, I can tell." I nodded at the trampoline and grinned.

"Come jump with me!" She pulled me by the arms until I climbed up beside her. "Come on! Jump!"

I couldn't get the right rhythm to match her jumping,

and I dropped onto my knees. You'd never expect a bouncy surface to be painful, but if you've already taken a decent hit to the tailbone in a night, any impact can give you a nice reminder of the injury. "Ow!" I gasped just as Cassidy came down again and I totally face-planted, and bounced on my stomach and face for her next few bounds.

But I could not stop laughing. It was impossible when I was completely helpless to stop myself from flying up in the air and flopping across the mesh. I floundered into Cassidy's legs, knocking her onto her butt again, and then we were both laughing as the springs ran out of energy.

"I give it a two-point-three. Tops," Neel said from the sideline.

"Boo!" Cassidy said. "The judge from Russia is totally biased!" Then she dissolved into giggles again.

"Hey, Heart," Neel said. "You really saw a fight?"

I lifted my head, spitting stray curls out of my face. "Saw it, *and* got knocked on my ass by stupid Amy Byers!"

"What?" Cassidy demanded, sitting up.

"Girl fight. Nice." Neel nodded, grinning.

"Are you okay?" Cassidy asked me.

"Well—" With a grunt, I managed to roll onto my back, panting at the moon overhead. "I'm not gonna lie, my butt hurts."

Neel snorted, and Cass giggled.

"But I'm okay." I waved a hand in what I thought was a very triumphant manner.

"Oh my God." Cassidy got onto her knees and crawled closer to peer at me through the shadows. "Wait—are you drunk?"

"No." I shook my head, and the moon jiggled in its orbit. I slapped a hand over my eyes.

"Oh my God, you are!" Cassidy laughed. "I've never seen you drunk! Neel, she's totally drunk!"

"Nice!" Neel repeated.

"You have to come with me!" Cassidy tugged on my wrist as she wormed her way to the edge of the trampoline again. She dismounted and beckoned wildly for me to do the same. I was a little less graceful, but I got off. Sometimes getting the job done is all you can ask for.

As soon as I was on my feet, Cassidy grabbed my hand and led me to the better-lit patio. Though calling it a patio was a little like calling the Statue of Liberty a figurine. It had an outdoor kitchen, a huge pool, a small building I could only assume was a pool-related structure of some sort, tons of loungers and chairs, and a fire pit on the opposite end from where we stood.

We ran into Ryan and Ally first, and Cassidy presented

me like a proud kid with a painting. "Look at this. Heart's drunk!"

"I'm not drunk," I said.

Ally laughed. "You are drunk."

I shook my head. Cassidy flagged over a few more No Drama people from nearby to show me off. Most of them laughed, or wanted to know where to get a cup, but I didn't know the answer. There were also a lot of exclamations over my finally arriving, and questions about what had happened to me.

"You actually sat in the limo with Troy and *got drunk?*" Schroeder asked.

"I'm not drunk," I said for the eighth time, shaking my head firmly.

"I can't believe you," he said.

I drew back with a pissy look. "Excuse me?"

"I just can't believe you'd be that stupid."

"God, don't be such a tight ass." Once the words were out of my mouth, I smiled. That had been a good response.

He glared at me. "Whatever."

"What's up your butt?" I blinked, realizing I'd made two references to his posterior in as many sentences. Time to expand your metaphorical language horizons, girl, I coached myself.

"It didn't occur to you that being incapacitated might be dangerous around Troy?"

I tossed my hand dismissively. "He was completely passed out. It was fine."

"There was no one there to look out for you."

"Um, hello? My *brother* was there."

He just stared at me for a second, then looked away, muttering, "Whatever."

"Hey!" I smacked him in the shoulder with the back of my hand. "Seriously, what is up with you?"

"Hmm, let me think." He tapped his chin hard enough that I could hear the sound his finger made against his skin even over the noise of the people splashing on the stairs in the pool and the music coming from hidden speakers. "Could it be that I tried to help you get away from your stupid date, but you just go back to him the minute your brother snaps his fingers?"

"It wasn't like that." I reached out to steady myself against the nearest chair.

"And then you don't even show up at this stupid party for an hour and a half—"

"What is the big deal? We ended up in the same place."

"We never would have come here if you'd just stuck with us."

"Us who?" I indicated the vacant space around us. None of our friends were in sight, having conveniently faded away as soon as Schroeder started getting bitchy. "Everyone else is having a good time except you. What is your problem?"

He frowned. "Nothing you need to worry about." And with that, he started toward the stairs leading up to the deck. But I wasn't about to let him get away that easily. I stormed after him. He was moving quickly, and I didn't catch up with him until he was nearly at the sliding doors leading into the house.

"Don't walk away from me!" I said, reaching around him to grab the handle of the door.

"Why not? You did."

"When?"

He held up one finger. "One. When you ditched me for prom to go with Captain Neanderthal. Two. When you let Phil dictate where you were going after the dance."

"Ditched *you*?" I leaned toward him. "Why are you taking this so personally?"

He opened his mouth, closed it, shook his head, brushed my hand away from the door handle, and walked into the kitchen without another word.

I wasn't about to chase him again. He was obviously in

some kind of snit that I could not possibly be responsible for. Fine.

I made my way back to the stairs and clomped down, feeling more sour than I had before I got here. This was supposed to be the point when my evening improved. Why was this whole freaking night so determined to be horrible to me? What did I do?

The area that had been a ghost town as soon as my fight with Schroeder started was suddenly crowded with a few of my friends in a tight circle, chattering like sparrows.

"What?" I snapped.

"Somebody's in a bad mood." Ally looked at me from the corners of her eyes.

"Yeah, Schroeder."

"Well, it seems to be contagious, Heart my dear," she said. "Have you seen you?" She indicated me with one long finger outstretched.

Refusing to obey her command to survey myself, I rolled my head and shoulders, letting them settle into a natural posture. "I don't know what you're talking about."

"Uh-huh."

Neel leaned toward Ryan, stage-whispering, "Should we tell her?"

"Tell me what?" I demanded.

Ryan shook his head. "I don't think she's ready."

"Maybe you're right." Neel nodded and leaned back beside Ally.

"What are you talking about?" I dropped onto the bottom step with a little too much force, and my head swam. Not that I was drunk, because I so was not. Probably.

"Nothing you need to worry about right now, sweetie." Neel batted his eyes at me.

"You guys suck."

Ryan cleared his throat. "Thanks for letting me take your ticket, by the way. I had a lot of fun with these guys." He tilted his head toward Neel and Ally.

"Aww, shucks." Neel made a big show of being embarrassed.

"Well, at least somebody had a good time." I propped my head on one hand. "I am so done with this night."

Neel pretended to check his watch. "Not even close."

I groaned, letting my entire upper body collapse onto my knees, turning me into a lavender tulle heap. "Seriously. What did I do to deserve this?"

"Is that rhetorical?" Ryan asked.

I looked up at him, trying to gauge his level of seriousness. Based on the smirk, I was going with "not serious." *Fais attention,*" I warned him in French, making him smile wider.

"*Moi?*" he asked.

"So!" Neel interrupted our little tête-à-tête, going cross-legged on the patio to look at me. "What are we going to do to improve your night, Heart LaCoeur?"

I blew out a sigh. "Suck the vodka out of my blood and tell Schroeder not to be mad at me. What did I even do to him, anyway? Nobody else hates me. You guys don't hate me, right?"

"He doesn't hate you." Ally sat down with us, crossing her legs and spreading the short skirt of her dress over her lap. "Far from it."

"Sure seems like it."

"Well"—she smoothed her dress a little more—"you *did* ditch out on the No Drama Prom-a." She gave me her slant-eyed glance again, showing that even she had a little resentment toward me.

"For a good cause!"

Neel snorted. "Sounds like it was a pretty crappy cause."

"Okay, but I couldn't know that."

"I was a good cause, too," Ryan piped up, joining us at last on the ground.

Guilt wrapped its uncomfortable tentacles around me, gurgling should-haves in my ear. "I know."

"Luckily, we were here to clean up your mess." Neel

patted Ryan on the knee.

I squinted at the action, distracted momentarily from my own woes by Ryan's smile. The gesture had been a little more personal than I usually saw out of my male friends.

Most interesting . . .

"And you *were* supposed to be Chase's ticket buddy," Ally continued.

"So?"

"Did it ever occur to you that maybe that wasn't just a coincidence?" Neel asked.

"No."

Neel sighed. "You're right. She's not ready," he told Ryan.

"Told ya." Ryan leaned in, nudging Neel's shoulder with his own.

"Not ready for what?"

"Oh my God, Heart, use your brain!" Ally threw her head back in frustration, raising her voice to a near shout.

I startled, leaning away instinctively.

"Easy there, Al," Neel said.

"Well, come on!" Ally went palms up, making the right one higher than the other. "Heart ditches out on No Drama Prom-a and doesn't show up where she said she'd be"—her hands switched heights—"Chase is mad at her. Gee, I wonder what could be going on with that? It's so confusing. I just can't figure it out!"

Neel and Ryan laughed, but Ryan leaned forward to make eye contact with her. "You are harsh!"

"Sometimes, you have to be harsh to get the message through." She tapped my forehead twice before I could swat her hand away.

And yes, like a complete idiot, I didn't get it until that moment. "You're not saying . . ." My jaw dropped. It actually dropped. I'd heard the expression for years. I'd even seen people do it on purpose, but I'd never experienced my own face falling victim to complete shock before.

"Hallelujah!" Ally looked heavenward and raised her hands in praise.

"You mean . . . Schroeder?" I twisted to look up and back at the sliding glass doors where he'd disappeared. I couldn't even see them from here, but something made me try. Primitive owl instincts, maybe. "Me?"

"Aww, it's so sweet when they learn to talk, isn't it?" Neel cooed, echoing Olivia's earlier teasing.

I couldn't be bothered with that now, though. "Are you . . . ?" I shook my head. "No."

"Oh, Jesus." Ally got up, stepping back to call across

the patio toward the fire pit. "Cassidy!" she called. "Lisa! Dan!"

The three people she'd called came over, with Marcus, and Becca from costume crew right behind. "What's up?" Lisa asked.

"Does Chase like Heart?" Ally asked, stepping back and indicating with her hand that they should address their answers to me.

"Yeah." Dan scratched his head, looking confused.

"Oh, totally," Cassidy agreed.

"Yeah, why?" Becca said.

"Mmm-hmm." Marcus nodded.

"Duh," Lisa said.

Ally let her hand drop. "Thank you."

"But . . ." I couldn't think of anything else to say. All I knew was I had an urgent need to deny them.

Ryan leaned forward, looking past Neel at me. He sighed and said, "I told you she wasn't ready."

Lisa made a dismissive sound. "Trust me. She was never going to be ready."

"You guys," I tried again, but my brain wouldn't form coherent thoughts. It was too filled with a buzzing sound of shock and too distracted by sending out all kinds of mixed signals to my body. I was both hot and cold at once, my muscles felt stiff but my hands were shaking, and my heart seemed to think I was running a marathon rather than sitting on the bottom step of Frank Blanchard's excessively huge deck.

Cassidy tilted her head like a bird. "You okay, sweetie?"

"I don't—" I shook my head. "I don't know."

"Can I go now?" Dan asked. "I'm up next on the pool tourney."

"Yeah, go ahead." Ally dismissed him with a wave.

"Does Chase know what you just did?" Becca asked.

"No." Ally shook her head.

"Oh boy."

Their words danced around my head like mosquitoes. It had to be a rumor. It couldn't be true.

Or could it?

"I gotta go." I jumped to my feet and rushed up the stairs, shoving open the sliding door and pushing my way into the noise and heat of the party. The kitchen was crammed with people, all watching something I couldn't see happening around the island in the middle of the kitchen. The crowd was like a solid wall of flesh, almost impossible to penetrate. Frustrated, I spun slowly, looking for an opening.

And just like that, I spotted Schroeder. He was back outside, only a few feet from the door I'd shoved my way through. I must have walked right past him. I squeezed my way back to the door and yanked it open just enough to slide through.

He saw me coming and started to back away, but I called out to him in a stern voice. "Schroeder. Wait."

"What do you want?" he asked.

"Can I talk to you?"

"If you must."

"Come with me." Snagging his sleeve, I pulled him toward the far edge of the deck, checking over the railing a few times to look for a spot where we couldn't be overheard by curious ears.

Schroeder tried to pull his arm away. "Where are you going?"

"I'm just trying to find somewhere quiet."

"This is fine." He gave his arm another yank, slipping free of my grasp. "What do you want?"

My heart was pounding wildly. I had no idea what I was going to say to him, so I blurted out, "Are you mad at me?"

"Are you still drunk?" he countered.

"No." The bomb dropped on me by my friends had been more than adequate to sober me straight up.

He sighed, his voice losing its edge. "What were you thinking, Spleen? Something could have happened to you."

"But nothing did. I'm fine."

"You got lucky, that's all. It could have gone way different. You already know that guy's not above taking what he wants."

"I know, okay? You don't have to lecture me."

"That was really stupid, is all I'm saying."

"Yeah, I heard you." I rolled my eyes. "Are you going to stand there and insult me all night?"

"You're the one who wanted to talk."

I was getting angry now on top of being nervous, which was not how I wanted this to go. I pressed my lips together and forced myself to take a deep breath before I continued. "Do you . . . like me?"

He crossed his arms. "Yeah, I like you fine. Usually."

"No. I mean, do you *like* me like me?"

His mouth went weird for a minute, twitching and jumping before he managed to answer. With a question. Of course. "What is this, fifth grade?"

"Schroeder. Come on."

"What does it even matter?" He faced the railing and ran a fingertip along the edge of one of the finials.

"I think I deserve to know."

He didn't say anything and didn't turn to face me. That was probably all the answer I needed, but I had to hear it. Out loud. In writing would have been even better, so I could read it over and over again until it made sense.

I decided to try a different tactic. "Please?"

He turned. "I am such a dumb-ass."

"What? Why?"

"I knew you didn't date. I knew you had all your weird rules about that stuff, but did it matter?" He shook his head. "Nope. I'm still stupid enough to—" His mouth shut, and he looked at me carefully. "Never mind."

"So you do?" I still needed to hear the words, no matter how much my persistence was irritating him. Which it was, I could tell.

Turning back to the railing, he said, "Yeah. Now, can we just not talk about this again?"

"I think we need to talk about it—"

"Why? There's nothing to say. You've got your 'Closed for Business' sign out—I'm aware of that. Let's just not talk about it, so we can get through chemistry for the rest of the year, okay?" He glanced back at me once, then walked quickly across the deck and down the steps, leaving me too shocked by his shutdown to stop him.

HEADS/TAILS

When someone hands you shocking news, there is never enough time or space available to accommodate it. Maybe there never would be enough time or space. Maybe that was life. What a terrible thought. Just year after year of perpetual shock.

I dropped my head into my hands.

Schroeder liked me.

It sounded so juvenile. Why is there no good word for having feelings for someone without using the word "love"? I'd always been a proponent of the word "crush" myself, but that was for my deliberately immature, unrequited crushes on fictional characters and unattainable real people.

I'd been the object of a crush or two in my short life. Freshman year, Scott May had asked me to homecoming. Thank God I was able to use the old "My dad won't let me go on dates until I'm sixteen" routine. Scott asked someone else and forgot about me, which was fine by me. It spared me having to turn him down with nonlegitimate excuses down the road.

It wasn't that I liked rejecting guys—I mean, obviously not, or I wouldn't have torn myself to pieces over the Troy/Ryan situation—but it was just easier to not date anyone.

Closing my eyes, I summoned the will to tell Schroeder things could never be *like that* between us. Ugh. I'd never had to do it to a friend before, and it sounded awful. How could I sit next to him in chemistry for the rest of the year if I'd flat-out rejected him?

For that matter, how could I flat-out reject him?

TAILS

Ryan, being a far better date than me, found me sitting at the top of the steps. I'd made it all of eight feet since I'd watched Schroeder run out of the music room. It was surprisingly secluded up there. The traffic was steady but light, and most people were just looking for a bathroom.

I was in the mood for wallowing, and most of the people who passed by seemed to sense that. I was being avoided like a puddle of vomit on the sidewalk. Except Ryan didn't seem put off by my vomitlike persona. He sat right down next to me.

"Oh man, you missed something beautiful," he told me.

I didn't speak, but looked at him from the corners of my eyes.

"Kim and Dan just came out of the laundry room," he said, like that was enough information. I hadn't seen either of them since the No Drama Crew rode over in the serial killer van together, now that I thought about it.

"Okay," I said.

"He had lipstick all over his face, and her hair was—" He approximated wild hair with splayed fingers around his head.

Maybe this was news after all. I lifted my head to face him. "For real?"

He nodded, grinning. "You should have been there."

I smiled, but tears welled up in my eyes and I had to look down. I should have been there. This prom business was definitely not turning out the way I'd imagined it at all. And as far as avoiding drama went, I was a total failure.

"Whoa, what'd I say?" He went hands-up like I'd pulled a gun on him instead of a few tears.

"Nothing. I'm sorry." I shook my head. "It's just . . . this night isn't quite like I'd pictured."

HEADS

Out in front of the house, the music was muffled considerably. I could hear the distant laughter of people in the backyard and make out a few glowing embers from the smokers farther out on the vast lawn. The driveway curved away from me, disappearing from sight where the guesthouse sat to my left. There were still lights on in the small cottage, and I wondered if the Blanchards were watching from the window, or if they were sound asleep, oblivious to the hundred or so teenagers swarming through their house. Part of me wondered if there was anyone in the house at all. Maybe that was where Phil and Austin had dumped Troy. I hadn't seen a sign of him since I got out of the limo.

Nobody was sitting on the low brick steps outside the front door, so I gladly took a seat there. I needed a few minutes to myself. Possibly a few days.

Behind me, the massive front door popped open, spilling music on me like a sudden rain shower. I twisted to look at my intruder, surprised that it was Ryan on the steps.

"Oh!" he said. "You're right here."

"Pretty much."

"I thought you might have made a break for it." He whistled through his teeth, lifting one knee like a sprinter in a still shot.

"Not yet."

"Can you spare some step?"

"*Mi steppo es su steppo,*" I said, patting the bricks to my left.

He laughed. "I think you should stick to French."

"Probably."

"So. I take it you had no idea about Chase."

"Not a clue."

"Really?" He wrapped his arms around his upraised knees. "Nothing?"

I shrugged. "This severely complicates things."

"Why? You don't like him?"

"I don't date."

TAILS

"He wouldn't believe me that there's nothing between you and me." I pulled hard on some carpet fibers on the edge of the stair, but they didn't budge. This was high-quality stuff. My dad would approve.

Ryan laughed. "He just thinks everyone finds you as irresistible as he does."

A shiver ran down my spine. "Stop."

"For the record, I told you he was flirting."

"Yeah, yeah. Lot of good your great wisdom is doing me now."

"You didn't tell him about me, did you?" Ryan peeped over his shoulder, checking the dim hallway behind us for signs we'd been overheard. He was like a spy for the gay CIA.

"Of course not." I sighed. "It was tempting, believe me."

"But you didn't."

I straightened up, looking at him. "No, okay? Jeez. What do you think he would have done if I did tell him, anyway?"

"I don't know. But bad shit happens to gay kids in high school."

"Ryan, for God's sake, you're not the only gay person at our school."

"Statistically speaking, you're probably right." He cleared his throat and flicked the nail of his third finger over his thumbnail. I'd heard the sound a million times during French exams. He was nervous.

I rested my hand on his knee and leaned close. "No, I

know I'm right. I know of two others."

He went pale. "Seriously?"

I smiled softly. "I get that you're scared, but seriously, if you want to stay in the closet, you could at least stand near the doors and peek out once in a while."

Narrowing his eyes, he gave me a little smirk. "You're not actually giving me relationship advice again, are you? I thought we'd already been over this part."

"I'm just saying you shouldn't be so afraid."

He nudged me with his shoulder, pushing me softly into the wall to my left. "Neither should you."

"I'm not afraid."

Ryan snorted. "Right. You are so afraid."

"Of what?"

HEADS

"I don't want to end up like my mom." I told him about her, and how having us had ruined her life. A couple of times, I found myself frowning in confusion, as though he should have already known what I was telling him. As if I could hear myself saying these same words before. I watched lightning bugs lift from the lawn as I talked, feeling almost hypnotized.

"So don't do that," he said.

I shook off the lightning-bug daze. "I'm not. That's the whole point."

"No, what you're doing is like saying 'I don't want to end up in a car accident, so I just won't get in a car. Ever.'"

"It would be the safest way," I tried to reason, knowing he had a point.

TAILS

"It's called birth control, Heart. Maybe you've heard of it? I seem to recall you sprinkling condoms around Taco Bell." He tapped his chin as if the memory were foggy.

"None of them are a hundred percent." Down the hall behind us came the sound of a flushing toilet, adding much-needed ambiance to this already high-class discussion.

Ryan shrugged. "Okay, then just don't have sex. You don't have to turn yourself into a nun."

"It's a lot easier to just avoid the whole situation."

"And how's that working out for you?" he asked.

HEADS

"Heart. Come on. You're already not like your mom."

"How do you know?"

"Because you've decided not to be," he said, as if it were

the most obvious thing in the world. "Because you don't even turn your back on your brother when he's being a dillhole. There's no way you'd leave your kids behind."

Suddenly, my eyes filled with tears. It was the word "dillhole" that did it. I knew they were tears about everything, but that's when my psycho body decided to go whole hog and start up the cry machine. I sniffed, dropping my face into my upraised hands again.

"God, I'm so pathetic. Why can't everything just be the way I want it to?"

Ryan laughed, the sound of it unexpectedly echoed by a few of the distant smokers across the yard. "It's good that you're keeping your goals realistic, Heart."

"I'm sorry. I wasn't expecting to deal with this."

He nodded slowly. "Mmm."

"What does 'mmm' mean?" I sniffled.

"It's just . . . how do I put this? Maybe it's just hard for me to imagine turning down something that's so much harder for someone like me to find."

"Oh." I cast my eyes down. "I guess I see your point."

TAILS

"Admittedly, it's not a perfect plan." I pursed my lips as I looked down at my dirty bare feet, wondering if I was leaving footprints on the cream-colored carpet. Nah, this stuff had to be top-of-the-line, with built-in stain resistance.

God, I really needed to stop spending so much time with my dad.

"But I'm not a nun," I insisted. "I've . . . been interested in plenty of guys."

"Name one."

"Johnny Depp."

He laughed. "Yeah, me too. How about someone human?"

I gasped. "Johnny is totally human. I will not have you talking smack about my man."

"Okay, someone achievable." Ryan stretched out, resting his elbows on the step above us and letting his legs lay along the next three steps below us.

A flash of Schroeder flitted through my mind. "All right. Paul West."

He frowned in thought. "The one who graduated two years ago?"

"Yes. Him."

"And nobody else."

I hesitated, pretending to listen when the music changed downstairs as a cover. "I didn't say that."

"Who?"

Narrowing my eyes at him, I said, "You first."

"We're not talking about me."

"We are now." I grinned at him.

He glared at me, waiting for me to cave, but he would have been waiting for a long, long time. I could hold out with the best of 'em. "Honestly? I think Neel is . . . attractive."

"*Attractive?*" I echoed, giggling. "You make it sound like he's a piece of furniture."

"I'm new at this, okay? I don't talk about it out loud." He wiped his forehead nervously.

"There's your trouble. Because Neel's one of the people I was talking about."

"You mean . . ."

"You couldn't tell?"

Ryan's face went still. "Unlike *some* people, I don't make assumptions about people based on their behavior."

"Ouch!" I put both hands over my heart. "All right, I get it. I'm being judgmental. I apologize, O great enlightened one who doesn't want anyone to know he might think guys are hot."

Before I knew what he was doing, Ryan swung his arm around my neck and pulled me into a headlock. I squealed, laughing and pushing against him, but my attempts were weak with laughter.

"Say uncle," he commanded.

"No!" I laughed.

He tightened his grip. "Say it!"

"Never!"

"Say, 'Ryan was right, and I should have listened to him!'"

"No!"

"Say, 'I have the hots for Chase Schaefer but I won't admit it.'"

"Ack! Shut up!" I gave a final push, and he let me go. My pin curls were stuck to my eyelashes and lips when I sat up and I gave him a crabby look.

He laughed. "Oh man, we are quite a pair, Heart."

Huffing hair out of my face, I sighed. "If you mean totally pathetic, then, yeah, I agree."

HEADS

In the brief pause between songs from the system around back, I heard crickets playing their buggy music. Blanchard's yard was probably a real oasis when it wasn't full of teenagers, I thought.

"Ryan, I'm so sorry I didn't say yes to you. I really should have. This night has been horrible."

"Well . . . yeah, you definitely should have said yes to me." He laughed. "But if it's any consolation, I've had a great time. In fact"—he leaned back on his hands—"I may have you to thank for some very interesting developments."

"Neel?" I said softly.

His cheeks turned red. "So *that* you noticed, but you're totally oblivious to Chase's raging crush on you?"

Now it was my turn to blush. "Your point?"

He laughed. "So. What are you going to do about this information now that you have it?"

I shook my head. "I don't know. I've never had to turn down a friend before. Not like I had to do to you, I mean."

"Who says you have to turn him down?"

"I—" I wanted to answer "I do," but the truth was, no one was saying I had to do anything. And even though I would have probably gagged putting it into words, there was a little part of me that didn't want to turn him down. It had a lot to say, that little part. I growled in frustration. "Why did this have to happen tonight?"

Ryan shrugged. "It's prom."

TAILS

Ryan slid closer when I sat up and put his arms around me—nicely this time—and rested his head on top of mine. "So, what do we do now?"

I shook my head. "I don't know. I can't even get Schroeder to talk to me anymore. He just keeps walking away."

"Maybe you should tie him up to a flagpole."

"And leave him for dead?"

He laughed. "No. I'm just saying he couldn't move that way."

"True."

"But then you might run away."

A soft laugh slipped from my lips. "I won't deny that's a possibility. So, maybe I'm hopeless then. What should we do about you and Neel?"

"Just because you put two gay guys in the same high school does not mean they'll be a couple."

"Oh." There I was, making assumptions again. I sighed. "Sorry. Prom is making me crazy."

HEADS

"Schroeder said prom was out to get me."

"He did?"

"Well, not really. He said I shouldn't let prom win."

"How's that working out for you so far?"

"Oh, fantastic. My date is unconscious somewhere, my dress is ripped open, my brother is being a total douchecanoe, and I just found out that Chase Schaefer has a crush on me. Oh, and he's pissed at me."

"Eh. Chase'll come around. He's just dumb."

I sighed, tipping my head back to look for stars. "About the only thing that hasn't happened to me is becoming the victim of a psycho killer."

Ryan burst into surprised laughter. "What?"

"You know, all those slasher flicks? Everybody dies on prom night."

"I thought that was only for slutty girls." He ground his knuckle into my shoulder.

"Oh, shut up."

"It's true. The good girls get taken prisoner."

"Great."

"Don't worry, though, they get rescued by the cops at the end."

"So, if I *do* get kidnapped and stuffed in the trunk of a serial killer's car, I shouldn't worry, because I'm a virgin?"

He grinned. "Exactly."

I gave him a shove. "Well, then you don't need to worry either."

"Tragic, but true." He sighed. "Come on, let's go find some other people. Be social. Try to stop being so pathetic."

"Actually, I think I need to talk to Schroeder again. If he'll let me."

"Maybe you need to tie him to a flagpole or something." He grinned.

"Yeah, or maybe stuff *him* in a trunk."

We laughed, and I took his offered hand, letting him pull me up, and gave him a squeeze. "Thanks, Ryan. You're, like, the coolest guy I ever didn't go to prom with when I had the chance."

TAILS

Suddenly, Ryan straightened up. "I have an idea."

"For what?"

"Nothing. Never mind. Just—wait here."

26 In which I throw beer at my brother and learn secrets

- -

HEADS

Looking for Schroeder had proven useless. The party seemed suddenly more crowded when I came in from the front steps. Always at least ten people between me and where I wanted to go—I couldn't see more than three feet in front of me. The lines outside all four of the bathrooms I came across were ridiculous, so I didn't think he'd managed to escape into one of them, but I couldn't know that for sure.

I didn't even know why exactly I was trying to find him, since I had no clue what I'd say when I found him. All I knew was that I'd hurt him, and I needed to fix it.

Frustration had my teeth clenched and tears pricking at the backs of my eyes as I searched. The last thing I wanted to do was cry again tonight, but it was starting to seem inevitable. It wasn't just Schroeder I couldn't find—it seemed like the entire No Drama Crew had disappeared. There wasn't even a sign of Ryan, who I'd just left on the front steps before beginning this stupid search.

So much for my grand escape plan. Schroeder had probably convinced them to leave without me. *Quel désastre.*

I decided to try back outside, and used an exit off the kitchen to start in the garage. There was a Ping-Pong table there, and I found Phil standing nearby, having a beer-chugging contest with Doug. I waited until he was done—he lost, incidentally—to ask if he'd seen any of my friends.

He laughed. "No."

"Damn it." I pinched the bridge of my nose against the threat of tears.

"They ditch you?" He laughed again.

"I don't know. But could you help me look for them?"

"I'm a little busy here." He made a drinking motion at Doug and said, "Let's go again. I can take your pansy ass."

"Yeah, right," Doug said.

"Phil, please." I tugged on his sleeve.

"Christ, Heart! Lay off!"

I drew back, startled. "Jeez! Sorry."

"You've been whining at me all night!" He took a beer from Doug's outstretched hand. "I don't know why the fuck I even let Troy bring you."

Suddenly my frustration coalesced into anger, and for the first time all night, it had a single focus. "You *let* Troy bring me?" I repeated. "Excuse me? Didn't you just hand me over to him like property?"

He rolled his eyes. "You're not gonna pull your feminist crap on me, are you?"

"Oh my God. That is so not the point. You're the one rewriting history—"

He completely ignored me, looking at Doug and cracking his beer. "Ready? Three, two, one—" The can of beer went up to his lips.

I stared at him in shock through three swallows, then swatted the can away from his face, sending beer spiraling across both of us like a sprinkler. Doug burst into laughter, spraying more beer onto us. The people who'd been watching the contest cheered. Idiots.

"What the fuck?" Phil snapped, glaring at me.

"Yeah, exactly!" I shouted. "What the fuck kind of brother are you?"

"What is your problem?"

"You!" I poked him in the chest. "You've been a

complete dick to me all night. No, not just tonight. You're a dick to me all the time! And I'm *done*." I picked up an empty aluminum can from the Ping-Pong table and threw it at him. It bounced off his left shoulder and spun wildly in the air before clanking to the floor. "Next time you speak to me, it better be to apologize. Otherwise you can just save your breath."

And with that, I whirled and forced my way through the gathering crowd until I burst out onto the driveway. Quickly darting around the corner, I pressed my back to the brick wall of the garage, glad no one was there to see me.

I was shaking. All over. I couldn't tell if it was a good, relieved kind of shaking, or the oh-no-I've-really-done-it-now kind. I pushed harder into the bricks, trying to remember how to breathe.

I'd never said anything like that to Phil. No matter how many times he'd teased me, or treated me like a second-class citizen just because I didn't want to be a cheerleader. Those times had always seemed like something I had to deal with to get the other times. Like when we'd joke together while making dinner, or all the hours we'd spent watching game shows together. That was the real Phil—wasn't it?

Another breath came out like a gasp.

This deep-breathing business was getting me nowhere. I pressed a hand to my mouth and tried to think what to do next. As far as I knew, my friends had already left, and I'd alienated my only other ride home.

Not the sharpest crayon in the box tonight, Heart.

Now seemed like a good time to let those frustrated tears have their way. I let my head thump back into the brick wall and closed my eyes. From the backyard, the distant sounds of laughter and splashing told me the pool and hot tub were no longer just being used for a little wading.

Then I heard my name. "Heart?" a female voice called.

I opened my eyes on an unexpected sight. It was Tara calling me, but Phil was with her. She had him by the ear, her fingers pinched around the sensitive cartilage like a giant earring.

"Heart?" she called again.

I was so startled, I stepped forward. "I'm here."

"Oh, thank God." She came closer, dragging Phil. "Your brother has something to say to you."

"Ow!" he protested. "Would you ease up?"

"No." She gave him a yank, torquing his head down to my level, but awkwardly angled. "Now, what do you have to say?"

"I'm sorry," he muttered.

"You don't sound very sorry." She twisted her wrist, and he flinched.

"All right, all right! I'm sorry!"

"What for?" Tara prompted.

"For being a dick to you, Heart."

"Good boy." She released his ear and he straightened up quickly, rubbing his ear and giving her a peevish look. "Now go sober up."

Phil looked like he wanted to say something to her, but thought better of it and went back toward the garage.

"Are you okay?" Tara asked me, squinting into the dark where I was still half-hidden.

"I'm fine. What the heck was that?"

She clicked her tongue. "I heard what happened in there. Nice touch knocking the beer out of his hand, by the way."

"Thanks."

"I'm not sure you've noticed, but your brother can be kind of a jerk when he's drinking."

"Mmm," I said, because I didn't want to tell her that he was sometimes a jerk when he was sober, too.

"I'm trying to fix it, but . . ." She shrugged. "What can I say? He's a slow learner."

"Why do you stay with him if you don't like the way he is?"

She sighed. "I love him. Don't ask me to explain."

"But why?" I felt disloyal, considering he was family, but I had to know.

Tara leaned against the wall beside me, looking out at the shadows of the trees in the side yard. "Because there's another side to him. And that side's pretty great."

"Yeah?"

"Yeah. He's so much smarter than he lets on."

"Do you know he's really good at trivia?" I asked.

She laughed. "I've noticed. And did you know he wants to be a teacher?"

"What?" Phil was about as child-oriented as a poisonous houseplant. As long as they left him alone, he wouldn't kill them. I could not resolve the guy who chugged beer with a teacher crouched in front of a group of five-year-olds reading a storybook in a soothing voice.

"He actually wants to be a coach. Like for high school football, but he knows he'll probably have to teach, too."

I blinked at her. That made a little more sense, but . . . "Seriously?"

"I know. See? He's a good guy. When he wants to be."

"And when he doesn't want to be, you just drag him around by the ear."

"Pretty much." She laughed.

"Doesn't that get tiring?"

"Sometimes." She tilted her head. "Tonight, yeah."

I wrapped my arms around myself with a sigh. "Boys suck."

"That they do," Tara agreed, sounding like it was the kind of annoyance a person just had to put up with. "Which boy sucks for you?"

"Schroeder." It didn't occur to me to call him by his actual name, but Tara nodded like she knew who I meant.

"And why does he suck?"

"Apparently he likes me."

"The bastard!" she gasped, dropping her jaw in mock horror. Why must everyone make fun of me?

"I know it's a little weird." I held up my hand to ward off further antics on her part.

Light dawned in Tara's eyes. "Ah! You're not interested in him."

"It's not that."

"So you are?"

I shook my head, even as the back of my neck prickled with nerves. "I don't know. I don't really do that."

"What? Be interested in people?" And there was that old familiar, what-is-wrong-with-you look I saw every time my no-dating thing had come up over the years.

"Yeah," I said shortly.

Tara laughed until she saw I was serious. "Oh, come on, you must have some idea if you like this guy or not."

"I try not to think about things like that."

"Aha! You said 'try.' That means you don't always succeed. So you obviously already know the answer."

My pulse pounded in my ears. I wanted to deny it so badly, but the heat in my cheeks and the sweat on my palms proved it impossible. Even though she couldn't see me very well in the shadows, *I* knew I'd be lying if I said she was wrong.

She obviously took my silence for agreement, because she said, "So, what's the problem, then?"

"It's complicated."

"It always is." Tara shrugged. "Just do yourself a favor and don't fall for one who needs as much work as your brother."

27 Wherein my friends pursue a life of crime, and I learn about sensory deprivation

----

TAILS

I stayed at the top of the stairs, just like Ryan had told me to. Not because I was obedient or anything like that. I just didn't have anywhere else to be. Weirdly, the volume of the music seemed to be going up even as there was less traffic coming by. It took me a bit to figure out there were probably fewer people in the house to absorb the noise. How long had I been sitting here?

Finally, I walked to the bottom of the steps and took a look around, reasoning that Ryan would still be able to find me. There wasn't much to see, frankly. The makeshift dance floor in the living room was sparsely populated, mostly with girls who seemed to be running on a reserve of sheer willpower. The dining room was empty, and the hallway looked like the aftermath of an explosion at a high heel factory, but that was about it.

I ventured to the front door, easing it open to do a quick search for Ryan in the front yard, when a commotion near the garage caught my attention. I stepped onto the porch for a better look.

A group of people were bunched together and moving quickly, though they appeared to be struggling with something. Like they were carrying a heavy piece of furniture or a rolled-up rug. I couldn't tell who was in the group as they headed down the driveway, but I could hear them whispering to each other loudly. Finally, they stopped at a boxy sedan, and I watched as they opened the trunk and stuffed whatever it was inside.

Were they seriously stealing something from Blanchard's house? I crept closer, trying to keep hidden in the shadows. I expected the group to get in the car and take off, but they stayed at the back of the car.

HEADS

I had no idea what time it was anymore, but my eyes were the kind of tired where blinking could have turned into sleep in a heartbeat. After my talk with Tara, I'd found a padded chaise lounge near the pool, and now it was starting to seem like a decent candidate for a bed. I hadn't leaned back. Yet. But sitting up was getting harder by the second.

"Heart!" My name startled me into opening my eyes (when had I closed them?), but I couldn't locate the source of the voice.

"Oh my God. There you are!" It was Cassidy. "We've been looking all over for you!"

"I've been looking for *you*." Well, I had been before I decided to throw a beer at my brother.

"I'm here." She did a ta-da pose. "Now, let's go!"

"Where are we going?"

"I have a surprise for you."

"You do?" I let her yank me to my feet and followed her as she headed for the side of the house. "Are we leaving?" I asked.

"Soon." Her Chuck Taylors made much louder sounds against the stone paths than my bare feet.

"What's the surprise?" I asked when we emerged onto the massive driveway in the front of the house. The brick steps where I'd sat earlier were still empty.

"You'll see." Cassidy towed me down the driveway until we reached a Volkswagen Jetta. Three people sat on the trunk—Lisa, Ryan, and Neel.

I felt like crying, I was so relieved to see familiar faces. "You're still here!" I said.

"Of course we're still here," Lisa said.

"I thought—" I shook my head. "Never mind. What's this surprise Cassidy's talking about?"

"Remember how you said your night could only end up worse if you were kidnapped by a serial killer?" Ryan asked.

I nodded.

"Well . . . we thought it would be funny to take your picture in the trunk of this car." He patted the fender.

"It'll be like documentation that you have officially had the worst prom in the history of proms," Neel said.

Laughing a tired laugh, I rolled my eyes to the night sky. "Sure, why not?"

"Yay!" Neel clapped his hands rapidly.

"Do you want us to rough you up a little bit to make it more realistic?" Cassidy did some fake boxing moves in the air.

"I think I'm roughed up enough, thanks." I could still smell a faint whiff of beer on my dress from when I'd knocked Phil's drink away.

Ryan, Neel, and Lisa slid off the trunk, and Lisa used a key fob to pop the lid.

"Whose car is this anyway?" I asked.

"Becca's," she said. "We asked around, and she had the biggest trunk."

I actually smiled at them, which was really weird considering what they were about to do to me, but hey, that's how you know who your true friends are, right? They're the ones who offer to stuff you in a trunk, and you're not only willing but grateful.

TAILS

Suddenly, Ryan came out the front door, followed by my brother and his friend Austin, of all people.

"Hey!" Ryan teased. "I thought I told you not to move!"

"You guys, I think someone just stole something from—" I started to say, but Ryan cut me off.

"Never mind all that. We found you. That's what counts!" His voice was overly jovial, like a game show host.

"Heart!" Phil called, holding his arms out to me. "My sister! Come here and give your big brother a hug!"

"What the—?" I gave them a crazy look but took a few tentative steps in Phil's direction. "What are you up to?" I'd hardly seen him all night, and suddenly he wanted to play happy family?

"Why would you think I'm up to something?" Phil asked, still holding out his arms. "Don't you trust me?"

I put my hands on my hips. "Not particularly."

"We want to show you something," Ryan said.

"What?"

HEADS

"Up you go!" Neel offered me his hand, and Ryan did the same, giving me two handholds for balance while I put one foot on the bumper and stepped up and into the remarkably empty space. I wondered for a moment if Ryan had said anything to Neel since our talk on the stairs.

"Her trunk is really clean," I remarked as I got situated inside with my fluffy dress doing its best to prevent me from doing so.

"We took a few things out," Ryan said.

"Aww, it might have looked more authentic if there were, like, jumper cables and an old coat or something in here."

"Please. Like a serial killer would leave you anything you could use as a weapon." Cassidy propped her hands on her hips, and I noticed her corsage was now hanging below her wrist and missing nearly all of its petals. "Now would you lie down so we can take the picture?" She held up her phone, doing a click-click motion with one finger.

"All right, all right. Give a girl a second, would you?" I eased my way down onto the fuzzy carpet, trying to baby my still-aching tailbone. Stupid Amy. When I was settled into a comfortable position, I gave Cass the thumbs-up. "Should I look scared?" I wondered.

"Nah." Neel shook his head. "Just go with whatever feels right."

"We'll take a bunch." Cassidy tapped her shutter button, and the flash blinded me. A collection of spots gathered in front of my eyes as she clicked away for a series of quick shots.

"How do they look?" I blinked hard, trying to look past the mass of after-burn on my retinas.

They were all gathered in close to look at Cassidy's display. "Looks good!" Lisa declared.

TAILS

"Just come here." Phil beckoned me again, and I took one more hesitant step. Phil's eyes went over my shoulder, and he said, "Grab her."

Austin, who had circled behind me while Phil talked, wrapped his arms around me, pinning my arms to my sides. "What are you doing?!" I shrieked.

"Calm down." Phil bent down to grab my legs, and I kicked at him. He dodged me easily and snatched one of my ankles out of the air. "Would you stop that?"

"What are you doing? This isn't funny!" I shouted. "Ryan!"

"Relax!" Ryan held up two hands. "I asked them to help me."

"With what?" I shrieked. "Let go!" I bucked hard, but only succeeded in letting Phil grab my other ankle. I was now suspended between two football players who probably weighed three times as much as me combined. I didn't have a prayer as they headed for the driveway.

"Ryan!" I twisted. "Help!"

"Stop screaming!" he shouted. "No one's going to hurt you!"

"This isn't funny!"

The sedan I'd been watching earlier loomed into view, and I realized the people loitering around it were all familiar. Cassidy, Lisa, Ally, Neel, Dan, and Becca.

"You guys! Help me!" I shouted at them, but they all just laughed.

"Oh my God, you have got to calm down," Cassidy said.

"Lisa!" I whipped my head as far to the right as I could, trying to make eye contact with my sensible friend. Lisa always had a cool head. There was no way she'd let them get away with whatever insane plan they'd come up with. "Lisa! What are you doing?"

She looked at Ryan. "We should throw her in the pool first to calm her down."

"No!" I screamed.

A muffled voice and some pounding caused Becca to give the trunk a solid thump with her fist. She laughed a fake laugh. "Never mind that. Everything's fine."

"You want us to put her in?" Austin asked.

HEADS

Lisa reached up with a smile and closed the trunk.

I let out a little shriek, startled by the sound and the sudden dark. "Very funny, you guys!" I thumped my hand on the floor.

"You okay in there? Can you breathe?" Lisa's muffled voice called.

"I'm fine! Just open the trunk."

"Not yet," Ryan answered.

The first trickle of panic settled in my stomach. "What?"

"We'll let you out in a second," Neel called, his tone impatient. "Just relax."

"What are you doing? You guys! Open the trunk!" I reached up gingerly, suddenly aware that I didn't know how far up the lid was, or what the underside of it looked like. Were there sharp bits of metal just waiting for some flailing limbs to chew on?

"In a minute!" Lisa called.

I could feel the panic growing, but I quashed it with anger. "This isn't funny! Let me out!"

Someone thumped on the outside of the lid and I jumped, just barely containing the urge to scream. "Settle down!" It was Cassidy's voice this time. "You'll understand in a minute."

"Cass! I am not okay with this! It's not funny!"

No one answered me this time, and I realized there was muffled chatter going on outside. I went still, trying to hear what they were saying, but they weren't talking loud enough. I reached up to the lid again with fingertips, feeling for a safe spot to pound my fists. If they were going to play kidnappers, I was going to play the most resistant victim who had ever lived.

Suddenly, a double thump came from outside, and I yanked my hands back in shock.

"Heart?" A new voice. Schroeder, if I wasn't mistaken, though he never used my real name.

"Yeah?"

The outside chatter got loud, and I could hear a few individual words, but none of it made sense.

TAILS

"What!" They meant the trunk, I knew it the moment Austin spoke. My dearest friends had colluded with my idiot brother, and they were about to stuff me in the trunk.

"Relax, it's really big," Becca assured me.

"Why are you doing this?" I tried one more time to buck free of Phil's and Austin's grips, but I just wriggled like a dolphin in a tuna net.

No one answered me as they gathered around the trunk, murmuring to each other.

". . . he's probably going to try to . . ."

". . . open it *slowly* . . ."

". . . hold him down?"

I watched as they slowly popped the latch and eased it open, three of them reaching in through the gap as soon as it was wide enough for their hands. They appeared to be holding someone else down.

Right then, I understood.

"Ryan!" I shouted.

"This is for your own good!"

"This is kidnapping!" I screamed.

"We'll let you out soon."

". . . the hell is wrong with you?" Schroeder's voice came from inside the trunk. "Let me out of—"

That was all he managed before Austin and Phil heaved me over the edge and dumped me in on top of him. Before I could even get out an "Oof!" the lid was shut again.

HEADS

"Make room, Heart!" someone shouted, and I heard the mechanical thump of the release mechanism. Before I could even reach for the lid, it opened, and my entire visual field was filled with something completely confusing. I couldn't make sense of the big shape overhead, but it was coming in fast.

I squealed and scrambled for the back of the trunk. I was almost clear when the shape thudded down beside me and the lid closed again.

"I'm sorry!" I tried to shove myself off Schroeder, but there were only so many places to go in the trunk of a Volkswagen Jetta. "Are you okay?"

"Yeah, I'm fine," he muttered quickly, before shouting, "Let us out of here!"

"Nope!" Cassidy called.

"You two need to talk!" Lisa said.

"No, we don't! Let us the hell out of here!" Schroeder moved suddenly, kicking at the trunk lid and rolling me into the wall with the effort. My head thumped against something hard.

"Ow! Stop moving!" I brought my hand up to rub the spot, smacking him in the face.

He ignored me, shouting, "Open up!" so loudly my ears clanged and I flinched. He tried to kick again, but all I heard was "Ouch! Fuck!" and he didn't make contact with the trunk.

"Stop moving!" I hissed, taking another swat at him. I made contact with something fabric-covered, so at least I hadn't hit him in the face again.

"Tell them to let us out of here."

"Open the door!" I called.

"Can you breathe?" someone asked. Phil. Aw, he does

care, I thought with an eye roll.

I considered the air inside. It was warm and still, but I felt like I could breathe well enough. "Yes!" I snapped.

"Okay, then. You're not coming out until you're friends again!" Cassidy called.

HEADS

"This isn't funny! Open up!" Schroeder shouted, and my ears protested the noise. They'd actually stuffed Schroeder in the trunk with me.

"Shut up!" someone outside shouted, and pounding rained down on the trunk lid. It came from all sides in a terrifying cacophony. I used my free hand to cover my ear and squeezed my eyes shut. Schroeder went still, too.

The pounding stopped, and a female voice rang out. "We'll let you out when you guys work it out."

"Work what out?" I shouted.

There was a pause. "Your differences."

"You're making each other miserable!" Cassidy this time. "It's just stupid!"

"And we're tired of listening to you whine." Lisa.

"And we don't want you to mess up the show." Was that Becca? I couldn't tell.

"So you can come out when you're ready to be friends again!" Ryan.

"Or more." Neel, laughing.

TAILS

"Does Ryan know you assholes kidnapped his date?" Schroeder shouted.

"Yes!" Lisa this time.

"It was my idea!" Ryan answered.

"What the hell is wrong with you, man?"

My ears were pounding each time Schroeder shouted, and I crammed my finger into the one I could reach.

Ryan sounded gleeful when he called back, "Nothing! What's wrong with you?"

"Why would you stuff your own date in a trunk? Are you sick?"

Laughter from Ryan. "Not at all. I've never felt better."

"Why are you doing this?"

There was a brief quiet outside, then Ryan shouted, "I'm gay, you idiot!"

"I *knew* it!" Neel yelled while my heart jumped into my throat.

Cassidy called out, "Now get to it!" with a pair of thumps on the trunk to punctuate her words.

PART 3

what are
the odds?

Prom Night (or, more
precisely, the wee hours
of the morning after
prom)

28 Concerning recent automotive safety developments and honesty

----

In the dark of the trunk, I shook my head against a sudden sense of vertigo. I felt like the car was spinning and dug my fingers into the upholstery for support.

"Are they serious?" Schroeder asked me in a hoarse voice.

"I think so," I croaked weakly as the world stopped seesawing. I didn't know what had happened, but I was glad it was over.

"This is insane."

He had no idea how insane. "I know."

"They can't do this. Wait—" He shifted beside me, pressing me hard into the wall for a moment. "Isn't there an emergency release? In case you lock yourself in the trunk?"

"I think you're right."

"Feel around."

I reached out with my fingertips extended, moving slowly so I wouldn't get hurt on anything unexpected in the dark. The inside of the trunk was remarkably smooth, all things considered. Lots of fuzzy carpet on the walls and floor, smooth metal and hard plastic on the lid overhead. I couldn't feel much, being crushed against the interior wall as I was, but I tried. Luckily, I was barefoot, so I even checked around with my toes, but there was no handle to be found.

"Find anything?" Schroeder asked.

"Nothing."

"Wait! I think I might have something. Check this out."

"It's pitch black in here. How the heck do you think I'm going to check anything out?"

"Put your hand on my shoulder."

I did as he said, barely touching his sleeve. He took my hand in his and stretched my arm across his body until I ran into the opposite wall. I had to roll onto my side and almost on top of him to reach that far, but I managed. Together we probed a small plastic piece, but no amount of pressure moved it.

"I think it's nothing," I sighed.

He sighed, too. "This car must be from before those latches were put in."

"They probably made sure of that." Our friends had

obviously plotted very carefully to make this idiotic plan come to fruition. In a weird way, I admired their dedication.

"This is insane," he said again.

"I know."

"Let's just tell them we're fine and they'll let us out."

I squished up my face in the dark, glad he couldn't see my efforts to sound normal when I spoke. "But we're not fine."

"Don't you want to get out of here?"

"Yes, but I also want you to talk to me."

Silence. Then he said, "This wasn't your idea, was it?"

"No! I swear to God. I had no idea what they were doing."

"Our friends are idiots."

"I think they're trying to help." And let's face it, they liked a good joke. Especially at someone else's expense. And this whole night had pretty much been a joke at my expense. It was actually a pretty fitting ending, all things considered. Now all I needed was an actual psycho killer to take the wheel and drive us off to his red room of pain.

"This is not the kind of help I'm looking for, *thank you very much!*" He raised his voice at the end so they'd hear him outside.

There was some giggling and a thud on the lid in response.

"They're not going to let us out," I said.

"Yeah, I got that. Thanks."

"Why are you being so rude to me? I didn't get us locked up in here."

"Neither did I."

"You're the one who's been acting like a complete pain in the ass all night. They never would have done this if we hadn't been arguing."

Beside me, he shifted angrily. "You're the one who ditched out on our plans. This never would have happened if you had just come along with everyone like you were supposed to."

"Yeah, and maybe I would have if I'd known you were going to be a complete baby about it when I didn't." Ugh. I would have so loved to cross my arms and give him my best evil-child-with-fire-starting-powers glare, but I couldn't even really get one of my arms free.

"I am not being a baby."

"Ha! Could have fooled me."

"You're the one who went crying to your friends about it."

"I wouldn't have had anything to cry about if you'd

just been nicer to me."

"Am I supposed to be grateful that you didn't want to go to prom with me?"

"You never asked me!" I shouted.

He sucked in some air, but no snappy retort followed.

Outside the trunk, more laughter confirmed that everyone was listening to us. Wonderful. I lowered my voice. "You never said a word. How was I supposed to know you wanted to go with me? I didn't even know you . . . liked me." I hated to say it like that, and I grimaced in the dark.

"Well now you know. Happy?" he asked.

"No."

"Yeah? Me neither. I'm so glad I told you."

My pulse pounded in my ears, and my stomach filled with mutant butterflies from Mars. These were not the gossipy kind of butterflies. These things had anger issues. It was now or never. I stretched out my pinkie until it touched his arm, which probably doesn't sound like much, but trust me, took a lot of courage. "I'm glad," I whispered.

He stiffened. "Because now you can avoid me?"

"No," I said quickly. "I—I don't know what to do about it, but I'm glad you told me."

"God, I'm so stupid," he muttered. "Why did it have to be you?"

I withdrew my pinkie in full retreat. If I could have, I'd have fled for the nearest hill. So much for courage. "I'm . . . sorry?"

"You're, like, the least available person I know. Why did I have to fall for you?"

The Martian butterflies chewed at my stomach. Best to fall back on my classic strategy of humor and sarcasm. Always a safe bet. "If it makes you feel any better, I can't seem to get over Johnny Depp. Talk about unavailable."

"That's not even—you're such a dork sometimes." There was a subtle undercurrent of laughter in his tone, and the Martian butterflies paused their war dance.

Summoning every drop of courage I could find, I stretched out my pinkie again, seeking his arm. When I found it, I brought my other fingertips to rest on his sleeve. "If I'd gone with the group as planned, would you have said anything?"

"I . . . don't know. I wanted to. I thought maybe—I don't know."

"If it's any consolation, I probably would have freaked out."

"Great." He sighed. "That makes me feel tons better."

"It wouldn't have been personal."

"I know, I know. Your damn policy."

"I've been informed that my no-dating policy may be a touch on the screwed-up side. Potentially."

Silence.

I chewed on my cheek, waiting for him to speak.

Finally he did. "I see. By who?"

"Oh . . . just . . . you know . . . everyone I know." I shrugged, though only one shoulder could go anywhere.

"What's the story with that, anyway?"

I sighed, and told him the background on my mom. It was weird to think he didn't know, but it wasn't something I talked about.

I didn't even think of her all that much. I certainly never thought of myself as someone to be pitied. Except for my name, of course. I didn't see myself as someone who lost her mom, because I never remembered having one. All I'd known my whole life was that I didn't want to do the same thing to my kids. But I viewed it the way I imagined everyone saw their parents. Like Lisa, who didn't want to be a teacher after seeing how hard her mom worked. Or Cassidy, who thought her dad was nuts for being into math and numbers so much he'd become an accountant. Like, on purpose. For me, it was just a little bigger. Don't start a family before you're ready, or you might end up running off to become a flight attendant. It seemed so simple. But maybe I'd gone too far with it.

"I'm sorry your mom left," Schroeder said when I was done. "That sucks."

"I don't miss her, or anything," I said, curling my fingers around his arm. "I swear. It's not like that. I'm not all damaged and heartbroken—"

"It's okay if you are."

"I . . ." My words stuck in my throat. "I'm not. I just want to do better. I know I can do better than she did."

"Well, obviously."

"I'm going to start by giving my children completely normal names. Like Mary and John."

He laughed. "I like your name."

"You call me Spleen."

"You call me Schroeder."

"Heart is a terrible name, trust me."

"It suits you. You're not meant to be a Mary."

"What about a Marilyn?"

"No. Maybe a Lung . . ."

I pinched his arm, which made him laugh, and then his other hand came over to cover my fingers. My toes curled, scrunching into the fuzzy wall at my feet, and my pulse tripled in an instant.

"Anyway, that's the whole reason for the no-dating policy. Just making sure I don't end up like my mom."

"So, as far as you're concerned, there's nothing in between No Dating and Having Two Kids Before Age Twenty?"

"Yeah, that's the part people don't understand."

"Count me as one of those people."

"I just figured it would be easier to avoid the whole thing than worry about how serious I was getting with someone. You can't get pregnant if you don't even have a boyfriend, right?" I swallowed hard, grateful for the dark so he couldn't see how embarrassing it was to talk about this stuff with him.

"You know that's not exactly how it works, right?" On top of my hand, his fingers curled and fidgeted.

"I was a lot younger when I came up with this policy, okay?"

He laughed.

It was time to change the subject before he started investigating my lack-of-dating history. "So, what's your story? Why didn't you say something to me sooner?"

"You mean besides the fact that you made it completely clear you weren't interested?"

I tried to pull my hand back, but he kept his fingers pressed over mine and even stretched out the fingers of his other hand until they brushed against my leg. Warmth spread through me from that point like I'd been touched by sunlight.

"I, uh, was kind of a big loser until high school."

"Huh?" I couldn't imagine him as anything but what he was.

"Let me put it this way—girls in middle school are a lot less impressed with a guy who can do ballroom dancing than girls in high school."

I smiled into the blackness between us. "Why did you learn, then?"

"My mom owns a dance studio."

Understanding dawned on me. "And she made you."

"Exactly."

"How did I not know this?"

"It's not like I go around telling people. I don't know what your dad does."

"He sells and installs carpet and flooring. It's pretty much the most glamorous job ever."

He laughed a little. "That's why he's got the van, huh?"

That feeling of vertigo swept over me again, and my ears rang. I squeezed my eyes shut, as if the darkness in the trunk wasn't already absolute.

"Yeah," I whispered when the feeling eased up. I didn't think sensory deprivation agreed with me.

"You okay?"

"Yeah." I opened my eyes, but there was still nothing to see. "You were saying about your mom?"

"Right. She swore I'd thank her someday. But some of the girls in my class took lessons there—jazz and contemporary and stuff. They didn't keep it quiet. Let's just put it that way."

I could imagine exactly the kind of torture they'd put him through. Middle school was not the time or place to be different. As someone named Heart, I was kind of an authority on the subject. It was weird the way you could be friends with someone but not really know the ugly parts of their lives. We all had our secrets, I supposed.

"I'm so sorry."

"Frank Blanchard was particularly unkind."

"Oh." And here we were in his house. Er, his driveway. No wonder Schroeder was crabby about the party.

"Add to it my piano lessons, and I wasn't exactly the most popular guy. I learned to keep a low profile."

"But now, you're . . . you." I rubbed my thumb against his bicep. "I think you're . . ." Why was it so freaking hard to give a genuine compliment? I could never think of a word that didn't sound fake or inadequate. "Well, you're . . . great."

"But not great enough to violate your policy," he said with certainty.

My heart pounded in my ears and my hand shook. I licked my lips twice before I managed to speak. "I don't know. I wouldn't say that."

His fingertips pressed hard into the back of my hand. "What?"

"I think—" I gasped in a noisy breath as my heart threatened to burst through my ribs. "I think maybe you're worth a change in policy."

He shifted, rolling onto his side to face me, forcing me to bring my knees closer to my chest with his pressed beneath mine. "Are you serious?"

"But you have to promise me some things." Spots danced before my eyes from the rush of my pulse.

"What?"

I laughed in a weird, gasping way, but it was all I could manage with all my breath gone. I had never been so scared in my life. "You have to promise you won't be such a pain in the ass."

His hand bumped once into my shoulder before landing on the side of my neck. Warm and not sweaty, like usual. Buzzing, electric heat ran through me, up to my head and down to my toes. "I really was being a jerk tonight. I'm sorry."

"And you have to promise we'll take it slow."

"Slow." His hand started to lift away from my neck, so I brought it back down with my own. I didn't want to lose contact. Even crammed together as we were, I needed the anchor of skin against skin to keep me tied to what was happening. I would have given anything to see his face.

"How slow?"

Blanking, all I could think of was my mother. I blurted out, "Well, like, let's not have kids anytime soon, okay?"

He let out a bark of laughter. "No problem!"

"Was that too much? I'm sorry, I have no idea what I'm doing. I didn't mean— I shouldn't have—"

"Heart."

My nerves subsided at the sound of him saying my name. "Yeah?"

"You're fine."

"Okay. I'm sorry. I'm probably going to be really bad at this, just so you know."

"It's okay. We'll take it slow."

For a long, heart-pounding moment, neither of us spoke. I was convinced he could feel my pulse beating against his palm.

"Can I ask you something?" he asked.

"Of course."

"Have you ever kissed anyone?"

I blushed. "Um, yeah. Remember earlier?"

"No, I mean, like, a real kiss?"

In seventh grade, before I decided to avoid all romantic entanglements, I'd been sent into a closet at Sophie Middleworth's birthday party with a passably cute boy named Dylan. It was Seven Minutes in Heaven, the most awkward kissing game in the long history of awkward kissing games. I vacillated between complete terror that we'd stare at each other and do nothing for seven minutes, and complete terror that he'd want to feel me up before the timer ran out. Eventually, he asked me if I wanted to kiss and I said yes, and we spent thirty strange seconds locked at the lips. He was more like a leech than a boy, sucking at my face like he was trying to extract my lifeblood. I was thrilled when the timer ran out.

Since my disgusting first kiss, I've shared two stage kisses with guys from school, one of whom was Neel, and once I failed to heed the warning signs of an impending kiss from an overeager dance partner at the homecoming dance as a freshman. Until tonight, that was it.

In answer to Schroeder's question, I said, "Um . . . define real."

He didn't speak, but pulled me close and found my lips

in the dark. There was nothing leechlike about his movements as he kissed me. My eyes slipped shut when he tilted his head, changing the angle of his mouth against mine. It was soft, warm, and made my fingers and toes tingle. Without a clue what I was doing, I parted my lips. He tasted like something sugary.

So this was what all the fuss was about.

I pressed one palm into his chest and fisted my other hand into the loose fabric at the side of his shirt. I wanted to pull him closer than our cramped quarters would allow. My breathing wouldn't slow down, and I dimly wondered if that was normal, but I found I didn't care enough to stop.

Finally he pulled back and tried to gather me into his arms, but our knees were still jammed between us. "We can stop," he said. "Slow down."

"No," I said. "Not that slow."

He laughed, and kissed me again, and I dissolved into it.

A mechanical wheeze and a click announced the trunk was about to open again, and we broke apart, both gasping in the cool air that rushed into the gap as the lid lifted.

Though it was the middle of the night, the ambient light outside was startling compared to the oblivion in the trunk. I blinked up at the semicircle of faces peering down at us.

"You guys okay?" Lisa asked. "We couldn't hear you anymore, so we thought you'd passed out."

"We're okay." Schroeder grinned at them, and I smiled and pressed a hand against my hot cheek.

"Soooo . . . what?" Neel prompted. "Do we need to lock you in there for a little longer, or are you ready to play nice?"

"Close it up," Schroeder said.

Cassidy sighed, making a move to close the trunk.

"Wait!" I held up my hand to block her from shutting us in again. "It was a joke."

They all looked expectantly as Schroeder. "Yeah, it's pretty stuffy in there. We want to get out," he confirmed.

"Sooo . . . ?" Becca was the one prompting us this time as I extended my hands to get assistance out of the trunk. "You guys are friends again?"

When both feet were flat on the blacktop, I turned to watch Schroeder climb out. My heart beat loudly and happily even as the Martian butterflies pirouetted nervously in my stomach. "We're good," I confirmed.

"Everything's all worked out," he agreed as he swiped his hands down his clothes, straightening them.

Everyone stared at us expectantly. I blinked back at them. "What?"

No one spoke.

I kept my eyes on them but leaned closer to Schroeder to stage-whisper to him, "I think they've gone into some kind of trance."

"Come on, Heart." He held out his hand to me, and I wove my fingers through his, smiling. "Let's get out of here before we catch whatever it is."

He walked swiftly, making me trot alongside to keep up, my bare feet making soft slapping noises against the pavement. Then, when we were only about four cars away, he stopped suddenly and pulled me into his arms to kiss me.

The cheering from our friends didn't stop, even after we did.

29 On the subject of naked women and juvenile pranks. And kissing.

The party, which had been confusing and crowded and annoying when I'd navigated through it earlier, now seemed almost inconsequential as I held Schroeder's hand and maneuvered through the backyard toward the pool. The No Drama Crew was at our heels, not that we'd told them to follow us.

Cassidy ran up next to me and smacked my shoulder with the back of her hand. I turned to shoot her a nasty look. She just went wide-eyed and pointed at Schroeder. "Oh my God!" she mouthed at me.

I tried to look angry, but a smile ruined my attempt. There was just no room for anger with all the darn giddiness rampaging through my system like a squirrel on Pixy Stix.

When we got to the pool deck, there were already

a handful of people in the water, most of them in their underwear. I wasn't about to go skinny-dipping, or even underwear-dipping, but soaking my feet seemed like a great idea, so I stepped down onto the first step of the underwater stairs in the corner. My eyelids slipped shut of their own accord, thrilling at the cool sensation on my feet, which had been through so much tonight. Too long in strappy heels, and too long barefooted on the various paved surfaces of Frank Blanchard's compound.

"Ooh, me too!" Lisa said, stepping into the water. With her shorter dress on, she was able to stand on the second step down without getting wet. Soon Ally and Cassidy were in there with us, while the boys sat on lounge chairs. Schroeder was the only one to take off his shoes and roll up his pants legs.

Before he could join us, Cassidy linked elbows with me and yanked me down to speak in hushed tones to the other girls. "Are you seriously going to go out with Chase?" she asked.

I looked over my shoulder at him, my heart hammering. "I think so. Yeah." It was all I could squeak out.

"Finally!" Lisa shouted.

"Yeah, yeah. Shush!" I hissed at her.

"Oh my God, this is so great!" Cassidy said. "He's

been into you for so long."

"I know." I blinked, feeling as if the world tipped and righted itself in an instant. It was like my brain was riding a Tilt-A-Whirl. I pressed a hand to my temple, as everything slipped back into focus. I didn't think I'd ever been this tired in my life.

"Wait—so did you like him, too?" Ally asked.

"I didn't really realize it—or at least I wasn't willing to admit it, I guess—but yeah, I think I did."

Cassidy and Ally went, "Aww," in unison while Lisa rolled her eyes.

"Hey," Schroeder said, coming down on the step beside me. His fingers skimmed the inside of my arm on their way down to hold my hand, and I shivered. This touching thing was going to take some getting used to. It was so much more intense than I realized it would be. "I cannot believe I'm standing in Frank Blanchard's pool."

"I know, right?" Ally said. "I so did not think we'd end up here tonight."

"I didn't think I'd ever end up here," he said.

"We were going to prank him . . . ," I said thoughtfully, narrowing my eyes.

"We were?" Cassidy asked.

"Were we?" Schroeder asked, squinting.

"I think . . ." A high-pitched whine drove through my ears, and I shook my head. "Wow, I'm getting so tired my ears are ringing."

"Somebody's talking about you!" Cassidy declared. "Which ear was it, right or left?"

"Both."

"Oh." She looked stymied.

"When are we going to Neel's house?" Schroeder wondered.

"Soon," Ally said. "I'm ready for some comfortable clothes."

"Agreed. Let's get out of here." Schroeder stepped back out of the water but kept hold of my hand. "We'll go find the others. You guys stay here."

I stepped back onto the pool deck and followed Schroeder, both of us now barefoot.

The only people we needed to find were Kim and Dan, and we were free to go.

"Weren't they playing pool earlier?" I asked, looking toward the basement stairs. "Or wait—weren't they in the gazebo—or were they?" I blinked hard, unsure which thing was true.

Schroeder looked at me. "You okay?"

I nodded, though I wasn't sure.

"Let's check the basement first."

We didn't see any sign of them in the basement, but Phil was down there with Doug, Tara, and Randi.

"There's my sister!" Phil shouted. "You all right, kid? You look like somebody stuffed you in a trunk." He laughed, and I felt another wave of dizziness.

I grabbed Schroeder's arm for support. "I'm going to head out with my friends. You guys okay?"

"Yeah, yeah. Go 'head. We'll probably just crash here tonight."

Looking around, I realized a few people were missing. "Where's Troy?"

Austin laughed. "Get this—Amy showed up all crying and shit—"

Randi rolled her eyes. "She wants him back, and he totally went for it. Pa-the-tic."

"Oh!" I wasn't sure if I felt relieved or disappointed in him. "Well . . . okay, I guess."

Tara got up suddenly and gave me a little hug. "I had fun with you tonight."

I got a confusing series of flashes—Tara's dress sparkling in afternoon sunlight, crowning of prom court, watching her dance with my brother, standing in the shadows outside Blanchard's house.

"Me too," I said, because it seemed to be the right thing to say.

I waved to everybody as Schroeder headed back toward the stairs.

"Hey, Heart, wait a second!" Phil called after me. I slowed and turned back to face him. "This guy somebody I need to know about?" he asked, nodding at Schroeder and trying to look intimidating.

"Oh please, Phil." I rolled my eyes.

"Be good to my sister," he said, poking his finger out at poor Schroeder.

"And you be good to Tara," I replied, jabbing my finger into his chest. "Maybe lay off the booze tonight, huh? She shouldn't have to take care of you all the time."

"Yeah, yeah." He sounded dismissive, but then he looked me in the eye. "All right."

"I'll take Personal Growth for two hundred, Alex," I teased.

"Same to you."

"See you at home." I grinned at him and turned to follow Schroeder out of the basement.

"What was that about?" he asked as we squeezed up the crowded steps.

"Long story. I'll tell you sometime."

We surveyed the main floor and didn't find any sign of our missing No Drama Crew members.

"Upstairs?" Schroeder asked doubtfully.

"We should check."

Most of the rooms on the upper floor were closed, just like last time I was up here, but this time not all of them seemed to be occupied. We opened most of the doors, coming across several unconscious people. It was impossible to tell if they were sleeping or passed out, and I was well beyond the point where I wanted to be responsible for anyone who'd overindulged.

The last room we checked had a sign on it that said KEEP OUT, OR I'LL KILL YOU.

"Call me crazy, but I'm guessing this is Frank's room," I said.

"Five bucks says he has at least one poster of a naked chick on his wall."

"Eww."

"Wanna find out?" Schroeder had a wicked gleam in his eye that could not be denied.

"Let's go." I popped the handle, surprised it wasn't locked. Apparently, Frank Blanchard believed his word was sufficient deterrent. Inside, the only glow came from a fish tank. Except when we got closer, I realized it was actually home to a large lizard of some sort.

I couldn't help it. "Gross," I said with a shudder.

"Huh. I would have thought you were an animal lover," Schroeder said.

"Furry ones? Yes. Scaly ones? No."

He smiled and let go of my hand to circle the room quickly. I found myself staring at the lizard's bulging eyes, unable to look away.

"Aha!" Schroeder pushed the main door shut, revealing the predicted poster of a busty blonde on the wall.

"That's just sad," I declared.

"Sad?"

"Well, it's so predictable. Why do guys like blondes with impossible proportions?" I held my hands out to indicate the size of boobs I'd need to compare to Little Miss Naked.

"I prefer brunettes myself," he said.

I rolled my eyes. "What a line."

"It's true!" He closed the distance between us and put his hands on my hips. "There's just something about dark brown hair that I like. . . ." He kissed me then, and it was the first time we didn't have an audience or a tight space to contend with. We came together, my arms sliding along his shoulders and his around my waist, breathing in sync as our lips moved together.

All over my body, nerve endings fired to life, bringing sensations back to my brain in a wild flurry. I pressed myself so hard into him that he stepped back for balance. It happened again and again until he bumped into Blanchard's bed. We sank onto the plush blanket together, our hands and mouths never breaking contact.

Oh God, the things I'd been missing out on. Was kissing always this heady? This intense? I was dizzy with it, and desperate for more. I would have gladly kissed him until I ran out of oxygen, but he broke away.

"Slow," he reminded me. "You said slow." With a grunt, he pulled away, lying flat on his back and panting.

"Right." I held a shaking hand against my mouth. "We're supposed to be finding the others."

"Right."

But still, we both lay there breathing hard for a few more minutes.

"We should get out of here," I said.

"Yeah."

I got up first, checking for any wardrobe malfunctions. Beyond the obvious gap in the back where the tape was showing, of course. Schroeder was much slower to get to his feet, clearing his throat a few times and taking a deep breath before he stood.

"You okay?" I asked.

"I'm good." He looked around the room. "I'm strangely pleased with myself for making out in Frank Blanchard's bedroom."

I grinned. "Glad I could help."

"Let's go." He held out a hand to me, but I didn't take it. "What?"

"Let's short-sheet his bed."

"Seriously?"

Giggling, I shrugged. "Why not? You don't like him, right?"

He opened his mouth like he wanted to protest, but it turned into a goofy grin instead. "Yeah, okay."

Moving in tandem, we peeled back the blankets and quickly folded the top sheet. With the bed re-covered, there was no sign of the stupid prank, but we were laughing over it like this was the height of comic genius. It probably was.

"I wish I could see his face when he tries to get in," I said.

"I just wish there was some way of making him suspect it was me, but never actually be sure." Schroeder tapped his finger against his chin.

I considered the possibilities. "I could leave a Rolaids

on his pillow, like a chocolate in a hotel."

He laughed and held out his hand to me. "Come on, let's get out of here."

Hooking my fingertips on his, I followed him to the door. Suddenly, he stopped and reached into his pocket.

"Wait! I've got it." His hand emerged with a tightly folded twenty-dollar bill.

"What's that?"

"My mom gave it to me in case of emergency."

I rolled my eyes. "Way better than my emergency provisions."

Smiling, he let go of my hand to unfold the bill, revealing something inside. "To give it weight so it wouldn't fall out of my pocket," he explained at my quizzical look. When it was fully exposed, I recognized the gold Chuck E. Cheese token he'd lent me in chem lab.

"Perfect!"

He slipped back to the head of the bed and set the coin on Frank's pillow like a hotel mint.

We stole out into the hall, pleased that no one was there to witness our escape. Schroeder cupped my face in his hands and kissed me softly.

"What was that for?" I asked.

"I figure I should probably do that as much as possible

before you wise up and change your mind."

"Chase!"

He did a double take, fingertips still resting on my jaw. "Wow, that sounds weird."

"I'm sorry, should I . . . not?"

"No. I don't know." He smiled slowly. "I didn't realize I'd gotten so used to that stupid nickname."

"At least I don't call you Pancreas." I frowned at him.

He grinned. "That was one of my favorites."

I rolled my eyes. "Come on. Let's go find the others and get out of here."

30 On sunrises, cinnamon rolls, and fate

Time has a funny way of bending and stretching. Sit in a boring class and the minutes tick by so slowly you can watch your life draining out the door. But sit in the waiting room at the dentist and fifteen minutes will be gone before you can catch a deep breath.

Prom had spanned a lifetime's worth of hours for me, and yet it passed so quickly I could hardly believe the sky was turning pink with predawn light when the day-care-slash-serial-killer-mobile rolled onto the tree-lined street outside Blanchard's house. Neel's house was less than a mile away, but I could already feel my eyelids sinking toward sleep as I rested my head on Schroeder's shoulder in the back of the van. Our fingers were laced together on the seat between us, and his knee knocked softly against mine as we went over a bump in the road.

Hours earlier, I would never have predicted I'd end my night this way, and yet now it seemed like the most natural thing in the world.

"Neel? Will your mom let us sleep for a while before breakfast?" Ally mumbled from a row ahead of me.

"We should eat breakfast first, then sleep," Ryan said.

"This man is a frickin' genius!" Neel pointed at Ryan, sitting beside him.

Schroeder laughed, vibrating my head, and I grumbled, nuzzling closer.

"I am going to sleep until I'm forty-five," someone announced.

"No way. You'll have to pee before that," someone said.

"We're almost there," someone called from behind the wheel.

"Yay." Someone yawned. Their voices made a dizzying pattern in my head. I couldn't keep track of who was talking, or how much time passed after anyone spoke.

"We're here," someone said, and I tried to pry my eyes open. It was hard work.

"Abandon ship," Neel announced.

We struggled out with a lot of groaning and yawning.

Earlier in the week, we'd all sent bags with pajamas and street clothes home with Neel to stash until prom night,

313

and few things had ever sounded as welcoming as my soft pajamas just now.

Schroeder slipped his arm over my shoulders. "You look dead on your feet," he said.

"I feel like I've been through at least two proms tonight."

"I know what you mean."

Neel's mom greeted us with disturbing perkiness. She'd been up since four thirty getting ready for us. She sent us into two different rooms to get changed. Ally went facedown on the bed in the guest room we were assigned to as soon as she walked in.

"Get up." Cassidy nudged her. "You know you want to take off that strapless bra."

"I already took it off," Ally mumbled into the comforter.

"Where is it?" I asked.

"Don't know." Ally yawned. "Don't care."

"You guys, I need help." I turned, to remind them of my dress repair, and Cassidy started laughing.

"Oh yeah! I'd kind of forgotten about that." She came closer. "Oh my God, this has gotten wicked nasty."

"Just get it off me!" I protested.

Cassidy and Kim worked together, bracing their hands

against my back as they coaxed the massive placket of tape away from the fabric. Finally one side was free, and my dress fell in a heap around my feet, leaving me in only my bra and underwear.

"Holy crap, what happened to the zipper?" I whirled to inspect the damage. At some point during the night, the slide had come completely off the tapes. It was a miracle the tape held the thing together.

"You are so lucky that didn't happen at the dance," Cassidy said.

"No kidding." I picked up the poor, decrepit remains of my beautiful bombshell dress, taking in the detritus on the tape. "What is all this?"

The tape was a mosaic of fuzz. I recognized the color from the banquet chairs at dinner, the gray interior of Becca's trunk, and even some of the bronzy-brown plush that had covered Frank's bed. There were also bits of dried flower, a couple of seashells, a scrap of paper, what looked like part of a straw wrapper, glitter, a feather, and several things I couldn't identify.

"Yuck," Cassidy said.

"It's like prom threw up on you," Kim decided.

"Gross," Ally mumbled from the bed.

We got into our pajamas and headed out into the

kitchen, leaving Ally exactly where she'd fallen. There was no convincing her to move. The guys were already downstairs, we discovered, with glasses of orange juice and big cinnamon rolls.

"Neel, your mom rocks." I helped myself to a warm roll from the tray on the bar.

"She does, doesn't she?" he agreed around a mouthful of roll.

"Let's go to the dock."

We made our way down the wooden steps to the boathouse and circled around the side to the dock, walking out to the end, where we could all sit with our feet hanging above the water to wait for sunrise. The sky had a golden glow that promised we wouldn't be waiting long.

The prom postmortem began, with people sleepily recounting events.

"Did you see when Karen Lewis got pulled out by the chaperones? They had to call her parents and everything."

"Man, the look on your face when you saw Foley streaking!"

"Oh my God, I can't believe the people who won court this year. Talk about predictable. We have to change that next year when we're seniors."

"Yeah, good luck with that."

"Heart, I thought your brother would get king for sure."

"Nah, not with Austin and Olivia there."

"What was Olivia screaming about during dinner anyway?"

"It was a fake roach," I answered without thinking.

"Where'd you hear that?"

I blinked, getting that same feeling of the world tilting and righting itself. "I . . . saw it . . . didn't I? But, no . . ." I looked at Schroeder for confirmation.

"I don't know, you weren't sitting with us," he reminded me.

"Oh, shut up." I nudged him with my shoulder. "Are you ever going to let that go?"

"Nope. You owe me one prom."

"Maybe if you'd actually ask me, I'd go with you."

"Heart, will you go to prom with me?"

"When? Next year?"

"I'm pretty sure that's the next one, yeah."

"Ow-ow-owww!" Cassidy howled. "Chase Schaefer— makin' his move!"

"Ow-owwww!" Neel and Ryan joined her in another howl of approval.

"So?" Schroeder nudged me.

"You're really asking me to prom for next year?"

"Yes."

I looked at him with disbelief, but inside every part of me was screaming Y-E-S! What I actually said was, "Okay."

"All right then. It's a date."

"Ow-owww!" They all chimed in with howls of approval this time.

"You guys are idiots," I said.

The sun broke the tree line at that moment, with its first bright sliver. We all fell silent, and the birds burst into delighted song.

Schroeder—Chase—put his arm around my waist, and I let my hand rest on his knee. Down the row, Cassidy sighed contentedly.

"This is good," she said.

"Very good," Dan agreed.

"Thanks for adopting me tonight, you guys," Ryan said softly.

"It wouldn't have been the same without you." Neel slid his leg closer and hooked his foot behind Ryan's ankle.

The sun still had some rising to do, but I didn't get to see the rest, since Chase decided he should kiss me. Dizziness swept through me as my overtired body tried to process the delicious feeling of his lips against mine. I couldn't seem to piece together everything that had led to this moment, but I knew I didn't belong anywhere else.

Maybe, just maybe, there's such a thing as fate after all?

Acknowledgments

Many thanks to the people who helped me to deliver Heart's story to your hands. To everyone at HarperTeen who took a chance on a first-time novelist, especially Erica Sussman, editor extraordinaire and fearless anti-ellipses warrior. To super agent Laura Bradford, for patience, tough love, and handling all the scary bits of the publishing world.

My critique partners are the best, and I can't imagine doing this without them. To Jessica Souders, for your incomparable insights, for always being my personal field guide, and for believing I'd make it to this point even when I didn't. I would definitely not have made it this far without you. And to Heather Whitley, who could start a practice as a professional character therapist. Your enthusiasm and encouragement always bolster my courage.

To the Wednesday night Barnes & Noble crew for keeping a fire lit under my bum and squeeing every step of the way. To the Inkslingers, especially MJ Heiser, James McShane, Nancy Keel, Ryan Hunter, and John Crumpley, without whom I would probably still be hiding behind a silly screen name, afraid to put myself out there. And to my many writing friends on-line and off-, who inspire and encourage me whether or not they know it.

To my family, especially Lindsay Maruszewski, my number-one cheerleader. My mom, who gave me a love of books, my stepfather, who supports everything I have ever done without hesitation. And everyone else in my family who reacted to my desire to be a writer with "Of course!" and "How can we help?" Thank you for always always always believing in me.

To Jack, thank you for being patient with me when I have to do writing work. Someday you'll be old enough to read this book, I promise. And to Joe, for always treating me like I was a pro. Thank you for so many carry-out dinners, taking the kiddo when I needed time, gold medal–worthy financial gymnastics, only thinking I'm sort of crazy, and being totally unsurprised every time we got good news. Maybe someday I'll let you read my book.

LOOK OUT FOR:

AUTHOR OF ASK AGAIN LATER

TOP
TEN
CLUES
you're
CLUELESS

LIZ CZUKAS

TOP FIVE THINGS THAT ARE RUINING CHLOE'S DAY

5) Waking up at the crack of dawn to work the 6:30 a.m. shift at GoodFoods Market

4) Crashing a cart into a customer's car right in front of her snarky coworker Sammi

3) Trying to rock the "drowned rat" look after being caught in a snowstorm

2) Making zero progress with her crush, Tyson (see #3)

1) Being accused—along with her fellow teenage employees—of stealing upwards of $10,000

Chloe would rather be anywhere than locked in work jail (a.k.a. the break room) with five of her co-workers . . . even if one of them is Tyson. But if they can band together to clear their names, what looks like a total disaster might just make Chloe's list of Top Ten Best Moments.